A Stitch and a Prayer

Other Books in the Quilts of Love Series

Beyond the Storm
Carolyn Zane

Tempest's Course
Lynette Sowell

A Wild Goose Chase Christmas
Jennifer AlLee

Scraps of Evidence
Barbara Cameron

Path of Freedom
Jennifer Hudson Taylor

A Sky Without Stars
Linda S. Clare

For Love of Eli
Loree Lough

A Promise in Pieces
Emily Wierenga

Threads of Hope
Christa Allan

A Stitch and a Prayer
Eva Gibson

A Healing Heart
Angela Breidenbach

Rival Hearts
Tara Randel

A Heartbeat Away
S. Dionne Moore

A Grand Design
Amber Stockton

Pieces of the Heart
Bonnie S. Calhoun

Hidden in the Stars
Robin Caroll

Pattern for Romance
Carla Olson Gade

Quilted by Christmas
Jodie Bailey

Raw Edges
Sandra D. Bricker

Swept Away
Laura V. Hilton & Cindy Loven

The Christmas Quilt
Vannetta Chapman

Masterpiece Marriage
Gina Welborn

Aloha Rose
Lisa Carter

A Stitch in Crime
Cathy Elliott

A STITCH AND A PRAYER

Quilts of Love Series

Eva J. Gibson

a novel approach to faith

A Stitch and a Prayer

Copyright © 2014 by Eva J. Gibson

ISBN-13: 978-1-4267-7252-8

Published by Abingdon Press, P.O. Box 801, Nashville, TN 37202
www.abingdonpress.com

Published in association with the MacGregor Literary Agency

All rights reserved.

The persons and events portrayed in this work of fiction
are the creations of the author, and any resemblance
to persons living or dead is purely coincidental.

Scripture quotations from The Authorized (King James) Version of the
Bible. Rights in the Authorized Version in the United Kingdom are
vested in the Crown. Reproduced by permission of the Crown's
patentee, Cambridge University Press.

Library of Congress Cataloging-in-Publication Data

Gibson, Eva.
   A stitch and a prayer / Eva Gibson.
      pages cm.—(Quilts of love series; 1)
   ISBN 978-1-4267-7252-8 (binding: soft back : alk. paper)   1. Quiltmakers—Fiction.   2.
Quilting—Fiction.   3. Families—Fiction.   I. Title.
   PS3607.I267S75 2014
   813'.6—dc23

                                                                         2013041876

Printed in the United States of America

1 2 3 4 5 6 7 8 9 10 / 18 17 16 15 14

*To my beloved husband, Bud, lifelong companion
and the wind beneath my wings,
now living in heaven with our Lord and Savior,
Jesus Christ.
And to my dear daddy, who welcomed him home
and who taught me to love
the old-growth trees of my childhood and the farm
near Wilsonville
where I grew up and still live.*

Acknowledgments

I would like to thank my daughters, Beth Niquette and Clytie Garretson. You encouraged me by first brainstorming and listening and then critiquing this story. Your observations and honesty mean much to me. I am proud to be your mother.

A big thank-you to those who encouraged me in my research on the history of the Tree of Life quilt:

- The guidance so freely given by the staff and volunteers of the Wilsonville Library.
- Allison Dittmar, assistant curator of the Old Aurora Colony Museum in Aurora, Oregon. The photograph of the Tree of Life pattern you sent and your guidance into its Oregon history helped me visualize the quilt I was writing about.
- Linda Machuta, manager of the Latimer Quilt and Textile Center in Tillamook on the Oregon Coast. Your photographs and information were exactly what I needed.
- I'd like to thank my brother Dale Nickerson for going through our family photographs and helping me remember the people and settings used in this story.

I'm grateful to Ramona Richards, my editor, for giving me the opportunity to be part of the Quilts of Love series. And for Sandra Bishop, my friend of many years and now my agent. Your love and encouragement is deeply appreciated.

To all those who caught my vision and prayed me through the chapters; you are too numerous to mention by name, but oh, how I thank God for you.

1

January 1899
Near the Willamette River
Wilsonville, Oregon

Whenever the wind blew hard and the rain came down sideways, lashing the windowpane, Florence Harms heard her dancing song. As the wind increased, so did the song. It sang of distant mountain peaks and torturous trails winding through giant boulders. It sang of sweat and blood, and always it climbed upwards, trembling from the heights, beckoning, calling; its strange haunting melody set her feet to dancing.

A part of her wanted to whirl, stamp, and lift her arms to embrace the music, to move in unison to the raging wind and the flutter of the flame within the lantern bathing the cabin's empty room in its soft glow. But the other part was fearful, her hand still clinging to the cane as her body slowly became more mobile, putting aside forever, or so she hoped, the illness that took her ability to walk and run freely, her energy to do her daily tasks.

The good doctor told her she had taken a turn for the better and she could expect to return to her full energy and freedom of movement. But it would take time. Will had returned from the icy north, and soon, even before winter ended, she would become his wife.

"Except I always wanted roses on my wedding day," she whispered into the silent room of the newly constructed log cabin that Will and the men from Frog Pond Church had banded together to raise.

The day after Christmas they felled the young firs in the grove along the back field and cut them into lengths the horses dragged to the site she and Will had chosen at the edge of the garden. It had only taken another few days to raise the walls and put up the roof, using shakes cut from an old-growth fir tree felled several years earlier. All they needed now was the order of glass windows to arrive by steamboat.

But would it arrive? Whenever it rained steadily, she remembered 1894, the year of the flood. Since then, from her home on the West Hills of Portland, she had always kept a close watch on the river whenever the rains refused to let up. Would there be flooding along the waterfront come morning? And what about the boats and barges? Would they be swept out to the mighty Columbia River and on into the ocean?

Florence pushed her thoughts away from the year when First Street had flooded and tried to recapture her song. She was in a safe place now, high above the creek that raced through the canyon during high water. No longer would she live in a tent; she'd be safe with Will in the cabin he was building for her.

Instead, there was a loud knock. She whirled around to face the door. Who would be out on a rain-drenched afternoon fast turning into darkness? Tilly? Her Aunt Amelia?

The front door blew open as she leaned forward on her cane and rose to her feet. "Will!" She gasped then smiled at the tall, broad-shouldered man with the worried frown. He stood on the threshold, water dripping off the brim of his hat and streaking his coat. She held out both hands, and he ran to her while her heart danced and twirled and spun inside her.

"Oh, Will," she whispered. She longed to reach up and caress his cheek with her fingertips, but he held her hands tight. She caught her breath. His tender smile put lights into his blue eyes, and the rough hands tightening over hers trembled. *Will, how dear you are.*

As the coldness of his hands penetrated hers, she stepped back. "Goodness, you're freezing to death!" She looked down. Mud spattered his trousers, and his boots attested to the heavy rain and thick garden mud stirred up by the horse's hooves and the men's boots.

"I can't believe you did this. Nobody knew where you were, not Tilly and not your aunt." His voice softened. "Besides, I—I wanted to be the first to show you our new home."

"I'm sorry," she said. "I just didn't think." Heat rose into her face. "I guess deep inside I'm still the little girl who wants to know what's wrapped inside the pretty packages. I just couldn't wait."

A sudden chill ran down her arms and she pressed closer into his arms, felt them tighten around her. "I can't believe you're really here. It's like I'm asleep and dreaming and I'm afraid to wake up."

"And if you are, I promise, I won't be gone."

"But what if—if you're not there?"

"But I will be there. And if I have to leave—for any reason —I'll let you know."

He bent his head and kissed her tenderly, deeply without holding back. "We're going to be married," he murmured as he trailed his fingertips along her cheekbone. "I know what it's like to want and have to wait."

"But what if I can't be the wife you need?" she whispered. "I'm tired of weariness and wanting to cry, sometimes without any real reason."

"But Dr. Rutler says not to worry." He gently released her and guided her toward the workbench someone had shoved beneath the window ledge.

"But I do worry," she protested, as she sank onto the bench. "Not so much for me, but for you. Are you sure we shouldn't wait until spring returns? Perhaps by then the warmer weather will ease the pain and swelling in my joints."

Will shook his head. "I have waited too long already. It's like I told you back then, in sickness or in health, I want you to be my wife. I still do, now perhaps more than ever. You are beautiful to me, just the way you are."

He took her hands in his and raised them to his lips. Gently, like the touch of butterfly wings, he kissed her swollen knuckles and then her wrist. "I love you, Florence. You are God's gift to me."

Afterward, he knelt beside her, resting his elbows on the window ledge, his chin cupped in his hands. "Have you been to the spring lately? It's one of the places I love most here, the cedars overshadowing it with their branches, the water dripping over mossy rocks into the deep pool surrounded by maidenhair fern."

His blue eyes darkened as he looked toward a place she had not seen in a long time. "I saw deer and coon tracks, even squirrels, and other wild creatures go there to drink. It's the perfect place. The creek below, and overhead more trees, giant maples and firs so tall they look like they're trying to touch the sky."

Florence smiled. "Don't forget the dipper tied to the branch. It's the first thing I saw when I pushed back the vine maple branches at the end of the path. It was like entering a safe place waiting just for me and gave me the feeling of coming home. And I was, but I didn't know it then." She sighed. "I wish I could go back there, but it's not possible. At least not now."

"But I could go with you, even carry you if you needed me to."

"But the rain," she protested. "Why, the mud on the paths would send us end over teakettle. Let's leave the water fetching to the young ones for a while. We'll take our turns later."

"I'm glad Tilly's here, especially this winter. She's a great girl. So is Hal's nephew, the redhead who's sweet on her. They make a cute couple."

"Yes, they do. I wouldn't be too surprised if they wed this summer. But we'd better get back to the tent. No sense worrying the family."

She paused as a worried frown creased his forehead. "It's who we are now, Will. Aunt Amelia, you and me, Tilly and her little sister. For better or worse, it's the way it is. We're a family."

"But, it doesn't mean . . ."

"No, it doesn't mean they'll be staying with us after we're married. Besides, Aunt Amelia has her own resources. And, yes, the girls do have their little place on the other side of the settlement. But they're all alone. Their father, even their aunt and the boyfriend she ran off with are still in the Klondike, at least as far as they know. They've had no word. Right now they need us—and we need them."

"But where will they . . ."

"Where will they sleep? They'll be in the tent. We'll be in the cabin." Her gaze wandered out the window. She could see the dark brown soil of the garden, the firs beyond, the road curving out of sight into the canyon below where birds sang in the spring and wild creatures lived and roamed.

"This window with the bench is my best spot," Florence confided. "I hope we sit here often, together, looking out the window, watching for spring, perhaps even put up a fence to keep the deer out of the yard. We can plant hollyhocks and heartsease when the soil warms."

Will got to his feet and again took her into his arms. "And your mother's rose." He gestured toward the open window. "Tomorrow I'll dig it up from beside the tent and plant it where we can see it from here. Of all the gifts we'll receive on our wedding day, the gift we'll treasure most will be your mother's rose."

"That and Mother's pearls." She laughed. "Just think I'll be able to wear them on my wedding day!"

Will smiled. "You haven't taken them off since I've arrived home from the Klondike at Christmastime, have you?"

"No," she whispered, as she slowly and awkwardly struggled with the top button of her coat.

"Here, I'll help you!" Will exclaimed. His hand came over hers, and he undid the button beneath her chin. Florence's hand slid beneath the collar, then around her throat.

"Will," she gasped, her voice hoarse with fear. Her stomach dipped downwards. "The pearls, I'm not wearing Mother's heirloom pearls. They're gone! I had them on this morning, I know I did: I saw them in the mirror when I put up my hair."

For a moment, her hands covered her face. "I can't believe I lost them," she wailed. "Almost more than anything, I want to wear them on my wedding day. And now, look what I've done! They could be anywhere, here, on the path, even in the tent."

Will reassured her. "We'll find them, Florence. They can't be far, they can't be. We'll look everywhere, spread the word. Aunt Amelia, Tilly, Faye; one of us is bound to find them."

He took her arm, and they walked slowly through the front room and into the smaller back room, pushing aside building debris and sawdust that lay across the board floor. It felt like it took forever. He reached for her hand, then with the lantern in the other, he guided her out the door, the faint fluttering flame their only light to push back the shadows.

There was no pearl necklace shining through the brown leaves moldering on the path, no tangled necklace caught in the underbrush grabbing at their clothing.

Tilly met them at the doorway leading into the tent. She took one look at Florence's face. "Are you all right?" She turned toward Will, noted the consternation written by the twisting movement of his lips, the worry in his blue eyes. "What happened?" she asked. "Where have you been?"

"Just over to the cabin," Florence explained. "I—I shouldn't have gone alone, but I did. Will found me there. And then I discovered the pearl necklace wasn't around my neck. She reached for her handkerchief and wiped away tears threatening to run down her cheeks. "We looked everywhere—the cabin, the trail, even held the lantern high to see if a stray branch might have grasped it up as it fell off my neck. But we saw nothing, it was getting too dark."

Aunt Amelia came up behind Florence and put her arm around her. "Did you have it this morning when you wakened? It might very well be here in the tent. If you want me to, I can help you look through your things."

"And if it isn't here, we can check the path again when daylight comes," Florence replied. "Oh, Aunt Amelia, I'm so sorry. You kept Mother's pearls when she gave them to you for safe keeping before the train wreck that claimed her life. I—I only had the necklace a little while, and already I've lost it twice— once on the river when the steamboat we were on collided with another. I'll never forget how awful I felt when the trunk with the pearls was swept overboard and disappeared beneath the water." Her lips trembled. "Now I've lost them again."

"Now, now, dear. No more tears. What is lost doesn't necessarily stay lost. And you know praying makes a big lot of difference, girl. Like you said, them pearls have been lost before, and not so long ago either."

———

As the rains increased and the waters of the river rose, the steamboats stopped plying up and down the Willamette. Will, anxious to find work after his return from the gold rush, found a temporary job in the feed store on Main Street, close to Hal's Mercantile. He even found a nearby boarding house, which was, as he put it, "a shade above sharing the horse and goat's accommodations."

The school remained open, and Tilly spent most days accompanying Faye on horseback, thereby increasing Aunt Amelia's and Florence's workloads. Tilly continued to bring a supply of water and wood into the tent to meet each day's need before she and Faye left. Nor did she forget to search for the missing necklace. She even donned Florence's cape and went out several times into the rain at daylight to search the path; then she searched the newly raised log cabin.

Although the couple had originally planned to have a simple ceremony in the tent, their plans changed when Mrs. Moad offered them the use of their home less than a mile away. "John is willing to fetch the four of you in our covered wagon—the same wagon John's great-grandmother came in to Oregon, actually to the same property where our house was built. His father finished the bedroom downstairs—there you can dress. It will be perfect. I can play the organ in our front room while the reverend comes in, then Will of course, then you in your white dress. What do you think?"

"I think it would be wonderful," Florence whispered. "But I still don't know when we'll be ready."

"Once these rains stop and the boats start running, you're going to be a beautiful couple," she said, and she was right. On the first Saturday in February, instead of the first Saturday in January as they had originally planned, the family was ready to depart for their neighbor's home.

A watery sun peeked out through the clouds and streamed over the tent as John drove his team into the clearing in front of the cabin. First Aunt Amelia, Florence using her cane, and Tilly came down the path.

"Now where did the child disappear to?" Aunt Amelia fretted. "She was here a minute ago, and now she's gone." She snapped her fingers. "Gone, just like that."

"She's coming," John said, "don't you worry none, she's on her way."

Even as he spoke, Faye exploded from the bushes at the clearing's edge, running as fast as she could toward them. "I found them! I found them!" she screamed. "Blue had them all the time."

"Why, child!" Aunt Amelia exclaimed as she held out her hand. But it was into Florence's open palm Faye laid the missing pearl necklace.

"I knew they'd come home," the child cried. "But why did the cat take them? I prayed and prayed. But why did God wait so long? I'd really like to know."

Tears blurred Florence's eyes as she held the creamy luster of the pearls against her pale wrist. The touch of the jewels brought her thoughts backward into the past. She reached down and pulled Faye close. "Oh, honey," she exclaimed. "I don't know why or all the answers, but I know some of them."

She looked up and her dark brown eyes met John's gaze. "When Will first asked me to be his wife, I said no. I loved him but couldn't marry him unless we had a house with a wide porch and white pillars. In my mind, I saw a house much like yours and Martha's, John." Her hand reached up and covered her mouth to hide the sudden quiver of her lips.

She took a deep breath and continued. "All my life my parents and us kids lived in one shack after another. When they were both killed in a train accident, I went to live with my older brother, Richard, and his wife, Opal, in Portland's West Hills. Even while I grieved the loss of my parents, the beauty around me, the gardens, my bedroom, even their parlor so filled with lovely things nourished my spirit."

For a moment, she covered her face with her hands even as Aunt Amelia put her arms around her. "Florence, it's over now. Let it go."

Florence lifted her tear-stained face to her family. "It's just what I am doing. You see, I loved Will, but I was afraid when he told me I'd have to live in a tent until he could build us a log cabin on the farm he'd just bought. I—I sent him away. I know now I would have regretted it forever if Aunt Amelia hadn't urged me to follow my heart and go after him."

Her gaze clung to Aunt Amelia's, and they both smiled. "You came with me when I followed Will to this clearing in the woods. But he was gone; he loved me so much he followed the gold rush into the icy north so he could strike it rich and build me the house of my dreams."

She turned and looked back at the tent she was leaving. "I haven't yet learned all I have to learn here, but one thing I do know: people are more important than things. There's even a verse in my Bible I'm learning from. I found it at Christmastime when Tilly and I opened the leather chest holding mother's pearls. There in the bottom of the leather chest was a secret drawer, and inside were little notes she'd written.

"When we didn't find the pearl necklace, I took out one of the notes and read a verse where she'd written the notation: 'my life verse.' I took the verse for my own, even memorized it when I was worrying over the pearl necklace, the cabin windows not arriving, and our wedding having to be postponed."

Aunt Amelia could keep silent no longer, "Well for pity's sake, child," she exclaimed, "what was it?"

John interrupted. "We need to get going."

"You mean Mother's life verse?" Florence asked.

"Yes," everyone chorused.

Florence lifted her chin, her voice came through clear and strong. "From Colossians, chapter three, verses one and two. 'If ye then be risen with Christ, seek those things which are above, where Christ sitteth on the right hand of God. Set your affection on things above, not on things on the earth.'"

"It's what I want my marriage to be." She turned and looked at each person standing with her. "You are my witnesses," she said. "You have my permission to tell me if I'm not living according to those precepts."

Faye grabbed Florence's hand. She smiled. "I think I understand a little bit better now."

When Aunt Amelia, Faye, and Tilly climbed into the back of the wagon, John carefully helped Florence into the front seat. His "we're off" echoed across the fields.

The horses lunged, the wagon lurched. Aunt Amelia, sitting on the bench John had nailed into place on the wagon floor for their comfort, leaned forward and gently touched the hood of the cape covering Florence's shining dark hair.

"May God bless you and the good man God has chosen to be your husband," she said softly. "And you will be blessed."

2

Blessed. I and the man I'm about to wed have been blessed.

The words Aunt Amelia had spoken warmed Florence's innermost being, even as the wagon tilted downhill and around the curve and they entered the canyon she had grown to love. Memories stirred by the lofty old-growth firs shadowing the grassy flats by the creek reminded her of the summer mornings she had struggled to master the scythe so Callie, their pet mare, and the goat who shared the clearing could have hay come winter. Just thinking about it made her shiver with weariness. With Tilly helping to transport Faye to and from school, it had taken both her and Aunt Amelia to load the wheelbarrow with the dried grass and push it up the hill and into the animal shed at the edge of the clearing.

As the horses' hooves clattered across the bridge over the water where she and Tilly had washed their clothes, she spotted a battered kettle that had sprung a leak and lay half-submerged beside the rising stream. The gray sodden ashes in the fire pit surrounded by bricks marked the spot where they heated the water for washing.

Yes, she and her man felt blessed. This was their land, their home, and now they had a newly built cabin all ready for them.

Chills of anticipation raced through her, then fear as the team started up the muddy, rutted road on the other side of the canyon as it rose before them.

John leaned forward and shouted encouragement to the horses. "You can do it, girls. Dig in those hooves! Keep climbing!"

The horses obeyed as they strained forward pulling the ancient Conestoga wagon up the sodden road. They stopped where the road leveled out and John hopped down. Florence smiled as she noticed his left hand pulling something from his pocket, then offering what was in his palm to first one horse, then the other.

"Like Will," she murmured, "he has a way with horses." She turned and smiled at Tilly and Faye. "And you girls have it, too. I've seen you with Callie and—"

"Eliza," Tilly said. "She's a beautiful horse, always ready to take Faye back and forth to school when we needed her last fall." She lowered her voice to a whisper. "John spoils his horses, keeps cut up carrots in his pockets. The horses love them."

The most difficult part of their journey was over once they reached Grahams Ferry Road and turned south toward the Moads' house about a mile away at the intersection where the curvy road crossed Grahams Ferry.

Her eager gaze searched the roadside for signs of spring. She spotted a clump of Indian plum shrubs sporting fresh green leaves, a tall willow leaning close to the road showing off tiny velvetlike buds at the ends of its branches. And the ferns—some of their fronds broken by winter winds and falling debris—waved softly in February's damp, cool air.

"Soon there'll be mayflowers and trilliums," she observed.

John nodded. "And Johnny-jump-ups. It's a bit early for those yellow violets yet, but they'll come when it warms a bit. We only have to wait."

They started down the hill, which led into the canyon where the creek curved through woodlands with a delightful mix of fir and cedar trees mixed with deciduous alders, maples, and smaller shrubs marching toward the river. "Water's pretty high under the bridge, but the road is good," John said. "Several of the boys living past your place loaded up a bunch of river rock and graveled the hills so the ruts won't get any deeper. It helps a lot."

Florence took a deep breath inward as the team neared the creek. As she leaned over to view the stream, she noted the water came up almost even with the bottom of the bridge.

"Now, don't you worry," John reassured her. "It's not quite there yet, nor is it going to be. Why, it's in the same place now as it was when I came over earlier. It would take a cloudburst before we'd be in trouble."

Florence smiled. "I can just imagine me in my white dress trying to cross the creek at flood stage. I'm glad you and Mrs. Moad were able to bring it to your house early on."

Faye's head popped up behind her shoulder. "What about me?" she cried. "I'm lots shorter than you."

"Don't be silly," Tilly exclaimed. "Why, the good doctor himself would put you on his shoulders and wade across to the other side. You'd be the driest one in our party, and Florence would be the one having the most trouble with her full skirt and white puffed sleeves filling up with muddy creek water."

"Oh, no," Florence lamented. "I should have worn the ivory silk blouse with the pink roses after all. But Aunt Amelia insisted—"

"For you to wear a white dress to go with your beautiful dark hair," Faye crowed. "And it worked! It's beautiful!"

Sudden tears stung Florence's eyes. She squeezed them shut, then blinked several times. "Just like Aunt Amelia said it would be," she half-whispered, "only it's so much, much more."

And suddenly she was remembering. Aunt Amelia had suggested a soft white cotton material for the wedding dress but she'd balked. "I want something I can wear later," she'd protested. "I really can't imagine wearing a white dress for everyday in the cabin or the garden either."

But Aunt Amelia had managed to convince her that a simple white dress with puffed sleeves and scooped neck could be dyed any color she wanted and wouldn't show the dirt either. In the end, Aunt Amelia purchased the material at Hal's Mercantile. It took all three of them to do up the seams by candlelight through the long winter evenings. In spite of her stiff fingers, Florence had done the best she could on the seams where her stitches wouldn't show, leaving the delicate work on the puffed sleeves, buttons, and buttonholes for Aunt Amelia and Tilly to do.

Faye's sudden shout brought Florence into the present. Their Conestoga wagon was turning into the driveway of the white house with two pillars. The horses slowed, then stopped in front of the wide porch.

"I'll help you up those steps," John said as he hopped down and onto the gravel. "But first we'll get our riders in the back out."

He held his arms out wide, but shook his head when little Faye appeared. "Stand back," he instructed. "Your Aunt Amelia comes first."

As Faye backed up into the wagon, Florence heard her voice proclaim, "Aunt Amelia, you're the queen! And he's waiting! You get to go first!"

With Faye on one side and Tilly on the other, the wide-eyed queen stepped into John's arms. Only instead of letting her down, he carried her up the stairs and onto the porch. Tilly and Faye ran after her and taking her hands escorted her the rest of the way to the door.

"And now it's your turn, Miss Harms," he said as he came back to the wagon where he swept Florence into his arms and carried her up the steps. He set her onto the porch and held out his arm.

Florence took it gratefully as they walked slowly across the boards. He opened the door, and with Martha on her other side, they escorted her into the bedroom where her wedding dress hung displaying its white glory.

"My dress! Why, it's beautiful," Florence whispered as she sank into the soft chair. "What did you do to make it so perfect?"

"Just a bit of starching and pressing is all," Martha said, "nothing more. It's a lovely creation."

"All the credit goes to Aunt Amelia and the girls. Without them—"

"John went to get your cane, and your aunt and the girls will be here in a bit," she said. "I'll bring tea for all of you. Your family won't mind sitting on the edge of the bed, will they?"

"We do it at home all the time," Florence reassured her. She looked at the quilt spread over the top of the bed. "Why, it's a signature quilt, isn't it? My sister-in-law has one from the time of the Civil War, and it's beautiful—just like yours. Did someone in your family make it?"

Martha nodded. "Actually, it was a gift from my mother on my wedding day twenty years ago. I usually keep it on the wall in our bedroom, but I wanted you to see it. You see, this quilt was created to honor my great-grandmother and great-grandfather's wedding. Although the signatures on it will be unknown to you, I thought you might like reading the

Scriptures about marriage those people wrote on the blocks. I hope you enjoy it and the tea. Having you here is my pleasure."

And she was gone.

When she reappeared, she carried a tray with a teapot decorated with tiny blue flowers and matching teacups. Florence's family followed. First, Faye clutching a honey jar, then Tilly with a pitcher of cream. Aunt Amelia came last, carefully balancing a small covered tray with shortbread and grape jelly.

Florence exclaimed her thanks as they placed the tea fixings on the table close to her chair. "You will join us, won't you, Mrs. Moad?"

But Martha shook her head. "This is your time," she said. "When you're finished, your family will help you dress."

It happened just the way she said. After they drank the fragrant tea and examined the handmade quilt, Tilly and Faye carried the tea things into the kitchen while Aunt Amelia helped Florence slip the freshly starched wedding dress over her head. She buttoned the tiny buttons adorning the front and adjusted the pearls Faye had placed in Florence's hand in the morning. "I'm so glad Faye found your mother's pearls. Your dress may not be the white silk and satin she envisioned, but they're perfect with the scooped neck. It would mean a lot to her to know you chose white for your dress. It was her dream."

"Even if it is cotton?"

"Even if it's cotton. It fits the neighborhood and the farm; it fits you and your dark hair and eyes. You positively glow."

A soft flush bathed Florence's cheeks as she bent to peer into the mirror. As she picked up the brush to put her hair in place, she glanced down at the hem of the dress. Her eyes widened. "There—there's a rose pinned to the hem, and it's pink!" she cried. Words failed her, and she clutched at the back of the chair where she had been sitting.

Aunt Amelia grabbed both of her hands in hers to steady her. "Oh, Aunt Amelia. I think I'm going to cry."

"Not on your wedding day, my dear." She stepped back and smiled at her niece. "If you do, I'll think you don't like my surprise."

"But I do," Florence exclaimed. "More than anything, I wanted a rose on my wedding day. A pink rose and—did you crochet it yourself, and when did you ever find the time?"

A sly smile spread across Aunt Amelia's face. "'Twasn't easy, but I found time. You didn't know I could walk and crochet at the same time, did you?"

Florence, her face warm and tender, put both arms around her aunt. "How can I thank you, Aunt Amelia? Talk about a surprise. All those walks. Why, I thought you were working on staying strong and healthy. You surpassed yourself on this one, my dear, and I love you."

She heard a knock on the door and turned, a frown furrowing her brow.

"You have a visitor," Tilly explained through the closed door. "Are you decent?"

"It's me," a deep, male voice responded. "I have something for you."

"Richard!" Florence cried. "He's my brother, Tilly. Oh, Richard, I'm so glad you came!"

Aunt Amelia stepped back as the man strode through the doorway and took his sister into his arms. After a huge bear hug, he stepped back and from his pocket pulled out a little sack of dried rose petals and placed it in her hand.

"Opal made it for you, because she hasn't been feeling well and couldn't come today. She was sure Will would return from the Klondike, so she harvested the roses from our mother's rose and dried them. Now you can smell roses when you say your vows to your Will. It's her gift for you so you might always remember."

Florence raised the tiny sack of netting to her nose and smelled deeply of the faint tantalizing smell of a bygone June. When she was alone, she'd slip it into her bosom to remember the fragrance of a promise kept.

Her Will had come back to her just as he had said he would.

⚬⚬⚬

Florence stood alone behind the closed bedroom door clutching her cane as she listened to the organ and the voices of the guests as they assembled in the Moads' great room. Soon the music would change into the triumphant wedding march, then Richard would return and escort her to where the reverend and Will waited.

She opened the door a crack, and as she did, Mendelssohn's "Wedding March" poured over her. She pushed open the door at the same time her brother Richard came toward her and reached for her arm. He put her cane against the wall and looked down at her as she stood still, her gaze caught by the lights in Will's eyes as he looked at her from across the room.

"You're lovely," Richard whispered as they slowly moved toward her man who looked so fine and handsome in the dark suit he'd borrowed from Hal. He stood waiting beside the Reverend Walton from the church. Florence even noticed several folk with their families from his congregation standing in the back, smiling encouragement.

Hal winked at her, and Irene wiped her eyes. For the first time she saw Clarence, Tilly's special friend with the bright red hair, standing beside Opal. A tear sparked her own eyes as she felt their love winging toward her. The good doctor, who had taken such good care of their family since they had arrived, quietly joined Aunt Amelia, Tilly, and Faye. As his hand gently touched the top of Faye's head, Florence felt a tear trickle down her cheek. Mrs. Moad pedaled and played the wedding march with fierce determination, her fingers flying over the keys. The air sounding through the reeds of the organ mingled with the melody, but no one seemed to mind.

As Richard put her hand into Will's, the organ stopped and a solemn hush fell over the room. The reverend spoke into the silence. "Inasmuch as we are gathered together in the sight of the Lord..."

For one wild moment, Florence wanted to stop the ceremony. *What if I can't be the wife he needs? What if I fail him horribly—will I become a burden? Will he leave me, find another woman to take my place?*

Even as her thoughts raced, she heard Will's words as he repeated the words after the reverend. "I, William Nickerson, take thee, Florence Harms, to be my lawfully wedded wife, to have and to hold from this day forward, for better, for worse, for richer, for poorer, in sickness and in health."

Florence's emotions choked her. Will was choosing her just as she was, in sickness or in health. *Oh, Will, I love you, I love you. We'll be together forever, as long as we both shall live.*

And then, quite suddenly, Florence Harms was Florence Nickerson. The people came forward to shake their hands and pass out hugs and kisses, while the sweet odor of hot cider invited the children kitchen-ward where biscuits, roast chickens, baked potatoes, and ham resided on the table. The counter was crowded with huge slabs of squash, loaded with butter, and a holiday assortment of pies, cakes, and cookies.

Martha and Irene handed out plates and created order as mothers and children filled them to the edges. The men slapped Will on the shoulders and made loud jokes about his new matrimonial state. The food gradually gathered them into the kitchen, leaving the new couple standing alone by the fireplace. Will's serious face bent low over Florence's creamy flushed cheeks that resembled the pink rose attached to the lace edging at the hem of her dress.

His blue eyes spoke of his devotion and commitment while Florence's heart whispered with unspoken words: *Lord, I need You to show me how to love in the forever way the reverend read about in Your Word before Will placed the ring on my finger. Something about love never fails, believes, and hopes and endures hard things. Lord, I'm weak. Make me strong. Give Will and me a love to last forever and ever. Amen.*

Will's words almost matched her prayer. "An everlasting love," he whispered. "One to go on into eternity." His fingers reached down and touched her lips. "I love you, Florence. Together we'll grow our farm and so much more. Together . . ."

3

Will and Florence drove the old two-wheeled cart behind Eliza to their new cabin sheltered in the trees. So slowly did they drive, John and Faye overtook them. As Will pulled the cart to the side of the road to allow John to pass, Tilly and Clarence stuck their heads out the back and shouted something about lovebirds who have so much to coo about, they forget to fly home to their nest.

Florence laughed and waved. Will simply raised his hat and nodded decorously while Florence wondered aloud where Aunt Amelia had disappeared to.

Will merely shrugged. "I think she went off with the good doctor. The last time I saw them, they were headed down the curvy road in a wagon filled with Frog Pond folk." He reached out and took her hand. "Now don't you start worrying about your aunt. She knows her own mind, and I wouldn't be too surprised if she and Dr. Rutler might tie the knot come spring."

"Or perhaps June when the roses bloom. It would be so perfect then. I wish . . ."

"We had waited until then?"

"Oh, no, Will, no. Today was so perfect. Besides, I had my roses." She pulled her long cape back to expose the crocheted pink rose next to the hem. "Along with this lovely rose Aunt Amelia made for me, Richard gave me a tiny netted sack filled with roses his wife, Opal, dried last summer." She took a deep breath and sniffed appreciatively. "I can smell them now. These roses petals are from Mother's rosebush she carried west with her."

"The bush I planted by our cabin?" he asked.

She nodded, and he continued. "I think I'd have liked your mother, Florence. She had an eye for beauty, and she bequeathed it to you, her daughter."

A warm flush mounted Florence's cheeks. "I like to think I'm like her. But, Will, she was more, so much more. She never complained about the harsh conditions she lived with, nor did she ever lose hope that one day she'd have a place to call home, a place where she and my father could set down roots. But it never happened."

"Did she share your dream—the white pillars, a big porch?"

"No, no, I don't think so. Why do you ask?"

"Just—well, I—I'd never been inside the Moads' home before. Today I saw it for the first time through your eyes. It made our cabin seem—how do I say it—crude and inadequate. No running water yet and small. I hope—"

Florence was almost sure she saw his lips quiver with emotion. Her stomach dipped downward in sudden apprehension. "But, Will—"

For a brief moment, his hand covered his mouth. "I—I'm not sure I'll ever be able to give you the beautiful home you so desire, and—I—I'm so sorry—so very sorry."

"Oh, Will, Will," she cried. "I'm not that woman anymore. Really, I'm not. Why, the cabin will be perfect for us. I mean it with all my heart."

She clasped her hands together as she searched for words. "That dream of the big house became more important because

I was so cold when I got sick in the tent and everyone had to wait on me. I wanted life to be different. But I'm the one who's different now. I really am. Part of that change happened with your Christmas surprise. When I looked out and saw you coming toward me in the snow, I thought my heart would burst. You were so tall, and the sunshine brought out the gold in your brown hair. I knew then I'd go anywhere with you. To the Klondike, even. We're husband and wife now, and we'll work together to make our dreams come true. I love you, Will, and nothing will ever change my love."

He reached for her hand. "And now we're going home to our cabin. Only this time it will be different. Someday I'll build a frame house, but first there's clearing to do to make room for wheat fields and pasture for our animals. We need a bigger garden with lots of corn, not just for us, but for the chickens, too."

"Maybe we can plant an apple tree next to the cabin in the spring." A wave of excitement flooded her and she almost bounced on the wooden seat. "Perhaps a cherry tree, too. It would be wonderful to have our own fruit."

"We might even be able to clear the back area just beyond the small swale where the pheasants hang out. It would be a perfect place for a vineyard."

He slowed as the road leading into their property came into view. "We might even begin by clearing out the property line here at the front, too." He waved toward the firs and maples crowding close to the road. "It would be a good place to plant a few fruit trees after we get it cleared. We might be able to build a frame house here one day. It's close to the road, and we wouldn't have to make the long trek through the canyon to get home."

"But I like the long trek through the canyon," Florence protested. "Especially in the spring and summer. Yellow Johnny-jump-ups, lavender mayflowers, white trilliums, and the ferns carpeting the hillsides, they're beautiful. And those tall firs guarding it all. I hope they stay there forever."

Or did she? As Eliza picked her way downward through the mud and ruts toward the creek, she leaned forward in nervous apprehension. But the mare made it safely down the hill. When she reached the grassy flats, she pricked her ears forward and tossed her mane, crossed over the bridge, and pranced triumphantly up the incline.

As they neared the top of the canyon on the other side, Will leaned forward. "There's smoke coming out our chimney," he observed. "Don't be afraid, Florence. I think I know why."

He touched Eliza with the tip of the whip, and she lunged forward. The mare didn't stop running until they pulled up in front of the cabin door.

He jumped down and came around to Florence's side. "I'm carrying you over the threshold, my dear," he said. "Hang tight to my neck and don't let go."

When he reached the cabin door, he pushed against it and carried her inside to a rocking chair she had never seen before—drawn close to the banked fire. He settled her onto the cushioned seat and leaned in toward her. "My own wife," he murmured, and the sweetness of his lips on hers was everything she had ever dreamed.

She reached up and smoothed his soft brown hair with her fingertips. "I love you, Will," she whispered.

He smiled then, released her, and got to his feet. "Your hands are cold, and I've been thoughtless." He gently touched her face. "There's winter chill on your cheek. Let me bring you a blanket."

He ducked beneath the blanket suspended in the opening between the front room and the room to serve as their bedroom. He was back in moments, his hands empty. "You have to see this," he exclaimed as he grabbed her hand and pulled her to her feet.

His other arm slid beneath her arm as he guided her across the room. When he pulled back the blanket, she gasped. The new bed constructed of rough, hand-hewn logs, which Tilly had made up earlier with fresh linens, now boasted a beautiful new quilt spread over the worn one they'd brought from the tent.

"The Tree of Life," she whispered, "my favorite. Who did this? Who . . ."

"Someone who loves you. And knows you, too. It has to be."

As they neared the bed, she saw although the quilt was similar to the one the ladies from the church had brought earlier to insulate the tent, it was different. This one had been pieced in shades of orange that were echoed in the long strips of fabric around the quilt edge. There was even a small white rose embroidered in each corner. Will was right; it had to have been made especially for them by someone who knew how much she loved roses. It had to be.

Will leaned over the bed. His big hands made rugged by outdoor work reached out almost reverently and touched the stitches. "They're so tiny," he marveled. "A work of art. How could anyone . . ." He shook his head in wonderment.

Tears she determined to keep unshed burned Florence's eyes. "I wish . . ." But the words wouldn't come.

"There's a block arrangement in a frame above the headboard," he said suddenly. He pointed. "Did you see it?"

Florence caught her breath as she looked at the wall. Her knees felt suddenly weak, and she sat down abruptly. The green blocks surrounding a close-up of the dainty white blossoms spoke hope to something deep within her. The promise of spring, of new beginnings, and a new life flooded her soul.

And it was Will who noticed the note tucked beneath the pillow. She took it, and her trembling fingers faltered, but she managed to unfold it and smooth it open. She read the words aloud.

"The quilting ladies of our Frog Pond Church pieced this quilt and blossom sampler just for you, Florence, and for your Will. May God bless you and bring you health and happiness and many years together."

She lifted her head. "Oh, Will," she cried. "It's signed by all the women. What a surprise!"

"I have a surprise for you, too. It's in the room we'll eventually use as our kitchen."

Once again, she reached for his hand. This time his other arm slid around her waist, and she leaned closer to him as they circled back to the front room and on into the area set aside for meal preparation.

As they entered, the homey odor of bread grew stronger. In front of the window, a table set for two complete with utensils and snowy white napkins on a red and white striped tablecloth welcomed them, as did a cast-iron pot on the wooden shelf above the fruit boxes that would serve as their drain board.

"Will," she gasped. "You couldn't . . . you didn't . . ."

"You're right, I didn't. But don't move." He bent over and snatched a napkin off the table. "My surprise is in the corner," he said as he put the napkin over her face and tied it securely at the back of her head. "Now follow me."

She moved forward slowly, clinging to his hand, and when he stopped, she stood still while he undid the knot. "You can look now."

She opened her eyes, and there, directly in front of her, stood a black cook stove with two lids with grooved holes and an iron handle designed to lift the lids.

"I wanted you to have this because you told me once you loved to bake. Remember those oatmeal cookies you used to make when you lived with your brother and his wife?"

He opened a big door on the side of the stove, and Florence leaned close. "The oven is beautiful!" she exclaimed. "It has a shelf in the middle and everything."

Her eager fingers tried to work the draught below the box to hold the ashes, but it refused to move. "This helps stabilize the heat in the oven. Oh, I do hope I can use it once you get it installed. I hope . . ." She spread her hands wide and looked at them helplessly as sudden tears welled up in her eyes.

"I'll help you, Florence. You know I will." Will changed the subject abruptly. "All I have to do now is put up the stovepipe. It'll be a cinch to saw a hole in the roof. I have a larger tin pipe with a spread-out flat bottom to go over the stovepipe. No rain will ever run down the stovepipe into the house."

Florence blinked back her tears as the sound of a screeching chicken assailed her ears. "Will!" she exclaimed. "The chickens in the sack. Our wedding present from the Moads, which John put in the back of our wagon! Something is after them. Hurry!"

She sank trembling into a chair while Will shot out the door. Through the window she saw Eliza plunge upward onto her hind legs, heard her neigh wildly. Then a runaway buggy with Will in hot pursuit plunged across the soggy garden soaked by winter rains.

She grabbed hold of the chair with one hand while she placed the other against the wall to steady herself as she made her uncertain way to the front door. If only she had her cane. If only . . . But there was nothing she could do, nothing to do, but wait and pray for Will's safe return.

The afternoon wore on and several hours passed before Florence met Will at the door, a weary disheveled man in a dark wedding suit covered with mud. He slid out of his shoes and left them outside before he came in. She opened her arms, but he shook his head.

"I don't want to ruin your dress," he said. "I'll get into clean clothes and then we'll talk."

"Eliza," Florence pleaded, "the hens? Are they all right?"

"The hens are gone," he said abruptly, "but the buggy and Eliza are fine. Tilly and Clarence have already helped clean them up, and Eliza is safe in the shed with Callie, even as we speak. Clarence gave her a measure of grain to cheer her up, and when I left, she was one happy mare. I'll tell you the whole story after I've changed."

Will was as good as his word. He returned to the front room wearing clean overalls and a blue plaid shirt. He went out and brought in an armload of kindling, then knelt to start the fire and chase away the lengthening shadows of early evening. Another trip and he brought back a couple of logs that he stacked next to the fireplace. He reached for the cast-iron pot filled with meat, small pieces of squash, and potatoes and placed it on the fire hook, turning it so the pot would hang over the flames. When he finished adjusting the pot with broad, capable hands still brown from the summer's sun, he pulled a chair beside Florence's rocker and sank into it. She reached out her hand and he took it.

"You are an unusual woman," he said. "Your groom abandons you, then returns in a ruined wedding suit and nothing much else, and you haven't even scolded him yet."

A saucy smile lit Florence's face. "She isn't going to either."

She turned to him then and noticed the weariness shadowing his blue eyes, making faint crinkles fan out at the corners. "You're tired," she said. "But I really want to know what happened, you were gone so long. Could we talk about it while our supper warms?"

He nodded. "I didn't know what was going on when I jumped into the buggy. Eliza was wild with terror, and I—I just hung on when she bolted across the garden and headed for the swale. She even jumped the stream flowing down through it. I was scared to death she'd break a leg and the buggy fall to pieces, but neither happened. Afterward, she responded to my voice and stood quietly, her sides heaving."

A rueful smile twisted his lips as he continued. "We just stood there together. I whispered into her ear about how wonderful a horse she was, and she seemed to understand. Once she calmed down, I climbed into the buggy, and I found the sack where the two hens had been was ripped apart. The hens were gone, but the rooster was still there."

"I—I don't understand. What could have happened? It doesn't make sense."

"It didn't make sense to me either. At least it didn't until I got back to the cabin." He paused as though uncertain of what to say next, and she jabbed him with her elbow.

"Go on," she pleaded. "Please, I need to know the facts. All of them."

He sighed. "As you wish. I just didn't want to put fear in you, but since you insist. There, close to where we embarked from the buggy, I found a paw print in the mud. I knew then what had spooked poor Eliza. It was a mountain lion, Florence, it had to be."

"But we've never seen signs of one before," she protested. "Or heard one either. Nor has anyone here ever mentioned they might be in our woods."

"I understand their territory stretches for miles. It's in the winter when game is scarce that they strike the farmers. I told Tilly and Clarence what I found, and they're making sure the shed is locked and all the chickens in. Tilly said she'd be over shortly to get our rooster and put him in with theirs. The poor thing—he's frightened out of his mind."

Florence took a deep breath. "He'll be all right. Tilly has a way with chickens and four-legged critters. Why, even the goat likes her—most of the time."

Will sighed. "What a funny way to spend our first day together. Those screeching chickens and me taking off after Eliza the way I did."

Florence smiled. "It had to be this way I guess, and I'm just glad you were here. If I were all alone"—she shivered—"I'd be scared to death, I think."

"I'll never, ever leave you alone for long, Florence," he reassured her. "If I have to go away even for a little while, I'll tell you first."

"Do you promise?" she asked as his arm slid over her shoulder.

He tipped her flushed face upward and whispered, "It's a promise."

"We need a love seat," she murmured as she snuggled as close as she could. "Do you suppose . . . ?"

He chuckled softly. "I'll put a love seat on my list, my darling. Until I find one, though, we'll just have to make do with what we have. Is it all right?"

"It will be perfect," she murmured. She looked up, saw a shadow pass the window, and smiled. Tilly had come for their rooster, and all would be well.

She lifted her face to his tender kiss.

4

Florence sat at the kitchen table, watching the white fog bank creep up from the canyon, her hot coffee cup enveloped by her hands. The sun was already visible, its strong yellow orb promising to burn through the shroud of white in its own time. She hoped it would be soon. But even as she watched, the milky sea swallowed up the horizon and the pale, blue sky high overhead.

The nausea she had felt for the past week began to subside. She took a cautious sip of the scalding coffee, feeling as if she wanted to return to her bed. At the same time, she wanted to stay awake and watch the fog surrender to the sun as it rose higher.

She sighed. If only Will were with her, it wouldn't matter so much, but he had left before sunup on what he described as "store business."

He'd held her close in the early hours before first light and whispered how much he wanted to stay with her instead of having to leave to take the steamboat into Portland. She took a sip of the coffee cooling in her cup and grimaced. Even though she was glad he was continuing to work at the feed store, she missed their leisurely breakfasting together. She wondered, did his frequent absences contribute to the uneasy feeling she felt in her stomach? *But I'd rather have it than pain and swelling in my joints,* she decided.

As spring slowly returned to the valley, her inability to use her hands had begun to disappear. Only occasionally at night did the old aches in her back and hips threaten to reappear. She'd get up and roll the bricks kept on the back of the cook stove into pieces of thick flannel, using them to ease her discomfort.

But the warmer the sun became, the less pain she experienced. It felt good to be able to do her own cooking, wipe down the table, and do the daily cleanup in the cabin. She had grown to love their small domain and the walks she could now take into the woods, sometimes with Will, at other times with Tilly and Faye.

Her thoughts turned back to their wedding and the first signs of spring: fuzzy willows and the tiny white flowers of the Indian plum tree giving way to fragile mayflowers and petite starflowers that sought the shelter of the mighty firs on the slopes down into the canyon. Then April was upon them with its satiny white trilliums gradually turning purple with age beneath the budding leaves of vine maples, alders, the occasional bigleaf maple, and the giant firs peppering the slopes above the canyon. Now May's golden buttercups and tiny white daisies dotted the meadows; the blossoms of the fading hawthorn trees turned to drifting snow as they joined the white snowballs. Whenever a light wind blew, their blossoms fluttered past, showing off the best of spring's bright glory.

She reached out to finger the fan-shaped conch she had removed from the bark of a fallen tree. Earlier she'd painted a mountain lion face on the smooth white underside. A small winged angel added in the background by Tilly's gifted hand reminded her even though she might feel lonely, God was with her. Somehow just putting the lion-like creature onto a harmless painting on a homely discard of the forest soothed her. It took away many of her fears as she walked alone in the woods.

She jumped as the sound of a knock on the front door interrupted her thoughts. Tilly's voice as she pushed open the door was warm and affectionate. "Are you up?" she called. "Have you had anything to eat yet?"

As Florence pushed back her chair, she started to reach for the cane she seldom used now. She drew back her hand and called out a greeting. "I'm in the kitchen. Come on in."

"I brought over some extra corn bread Aunt Amelia baked this morning," Tilly panted as she plunked a basket covered with a clean kitchen towel on the table. She sniffed appreciatively. "I smell coffee, too. May I have some?"

"But, of course." Florence started to stand, but Tilly waved her back into the chair.

"I can help myself. I'm good at it." She poured herself a cup and started to pour the remaining coffee into Florence's cup.

But Florence shook her head. "I think I've already had my fill."

Tilly nodded as she placed the pot onto the drain board, then sat down at the table. She sipped her coffee slowly, then reached out and cradled the conch displaying the mountain lion. "I didn't want to tell you this, Florence," she said softly, "but you need to know. He's back. I found his tracks between the woods and the shed where the chickens roost."

A cold feeling of fear swept through Florence. "When?"

"This morning. Actually, there were quite a few prints. I think—I think he might have been lingering there all night, waiting. Or something."

Tilly put her cup down abruptly. "I'm not going to let him have your little rooster." She lifted her youthful chin defiantly.

He sure does well with the other chickens—they're just one big happy family.

"But you have to be careful," Florence warned. "Why, you're more important to me than a chicken, I don't care how much you love him. You can't go out there at night! You mustn't!"

Tilly shrugged. "I've been thinking about it. I know where Aunt Amelia keeps our rifle, and I'm a good shot now. You know I am."

"Yes, I do know, but you can't risk it, Tilly. I've heard stories of mountain lions. I'm not sure if they're true or not, but I've heard they climb onto tree limbs above trails to wait for an unsuspecting animal, preferably a deer. They'll even take down a person if one comes by. When they pounce, they go for the back of the neck with a fatal bite. It can't be a pleasant death."

"But it could just be an old wives' tale," Tilly asserted. "You know I could be right."

Florence nodded. "I know. But what if you're not? How do you think Clarence would feel if he went searching for you and found your body half-eaten by a wild creature? I've been told mountain lions hide the larger carcasses they take down and keep coming back for several days just to dine."

Tilly shuddered. "What a horrible picture you painted for me, Florence. I wish you hadn't."

"I wish I hadn't either," Florence confessed. She pressed her hand over her stomach. "It's making me feel sick. And I haven't eaten breakfast yet."

"But you have to eat a piece of Aunt Amelia's corn bread," Tilly wailed. "She'll feel awful if you don't."

"Couldn't you take a couple out of the basket for me to have later? I truly do love Aunt Amelia's gifts from the kitchen." She leaned forward. "You mustn't go prowling around at night or even in at dawn's first light or the gloaming hours of dusk. You have to promise me, Tilly, please?"

Tilly nodded reluctantly. "It's funny the wild beast came right up to your buggy when you'd just come home from your wedding."

"It's like that with animals sometimes. People, too. They're curious. I sometimes think the mountain lion just wanted to surprise us on our wedding day." Florence shook her head. "Broad daylight, though, it's almost unbelievable."

"I think we need a dog," Tilly observed. "I've noticed more deer lately, and they might very well be a threat to our garden this year. Since your cabin is closer to the garden than we are, it might be good for you to get one."

"What does a dog have to do with the mountain lion?"

Tilly shrugged. "Well, they may not want to hang around where there's a dog. I'll talk to Clarence, see what he has to say."

And I'll talk to Will, Florence thought. But even as she put it into words in her mind, she wondered. Would he think she felt threatened because he'd been spending so much time away from the cabin? *But if I present it in the right way, he might not take it personally.* Aloud she said, "What if both of us get a dog? Might it be a possible deterrent in both places?"

"I don't know," Tilly said. She got to her feet and began to take the corn bread out of the basket and stack the pieces onto a plate. "Why am I doing this?" she exclaimed. "This is silly. I'll just leave the basket and pick it up tomorrow." She impulsively wrapped her arms around Florence. "Are you sure you can't eat just one piece with me? Actually, we could share one. Aunt Amelia need never know."

"No, she would never know, but we would." She patted Tilly's arm feeling as though the girl was her own daughter. "I think my stomach is starting to settle, and I have honey in the cupboard. Shall we warm a couple of pieces over the fire? There's still live coals, aren't there?"

Tilly nodded. As Florence got up to measure fresh coffee grounds into a pot, Tilly pierced two pieces of corn bread with a long fork and held them to the smoldering fire until a rich baking odor mingled with the coffee permeating the room.

Florence smiled as her stomach growled loud enough for both of them to hear. They both laughed until the unsought breakfast complete with fresh butter and honey materialized on the table in front of them.

"I'm glad you brought Aunt Amelia's famous corn bread," Florence confessed. "It's funny, but I think I might be just a bit homesick for the old tent even with the overcrowding and primitive cooking facilities. Can we do this again soon?"

"Absolutely," Tilly said. "I suspect I needed you just as much as you needed me." She took a big bite of the bread and grinned, which made her look like an adorable chipmunk. "Just being with you makes Aunt Amelia's bread more delicious than ever."

She swallowed and continued. "Now if we can find a couple of dogs to keep us company, it'd be perfect. It's spring, and surely someone nearby has puppies to give away. I'll pass the word at church and see what happens."

"And I'll ask Will. He might have heard something at the feed store about puppies needing new homes. We could even ask him to write a Puppy Wanted message on the blackboard in the front."

But even as Florence said it, she wondered if she really would.

By early afternoon, the morning fog had been blown away by a gentle south wind winging warmer air into the valley. Florence donned a light jacket and, with her cane in hand to steady herself over the uneven ground, went outside to view the open area on the side of the cabin where last year's garden had flourished beyond their expectations. Soggy from winter storms and late spring rains, it sported clumps of green grass in the very places where the three of them—Tilly, Callie, and she—had worked together to master the plow and turn the soil. Just remembering the hard work they'd done in order to have a garden made her shudder. If only she felt better.

Already the backs of her legs were beginning to ache, and she turned toward the cabin. She noticed then that the clouds toward the west were building above the low hills on the western horizon. *It'll probably rain before evening,* she thought as she quickened her pace. *The peas Will and I planted will love it.*

She smiled remembering the day in early March when the two of them had broken up the soil on the sunny side of the cabin and pressed peas into the damp soil. Already those peas were giving the cabin a lived-in look that she could perhaps perpetuate later with the yellow Johnny-jump-ups she'd seen blooming at the edge of the clearing where the tent stood. They would be easy to transplant and something she could do without fearing she might hurt herself.

The bright yellow gingham Will had brought home for kitchen curtains presented its own challenge. Would she ever be able to cut and sew the way her heart longed to do? *But I'm better. Really I am. Why, I painted the mountain lion's face on the conch. Tilly liked it, and she's an artist.* Florence could picture the material made into curtains with a matching flounce encircling the shelves holding the pots and pans. But her fingers still lacked the agility to hold a small needle, and using scissors did something bad to the joints in her thumbs.

As she neared the cabin, she looked back at the hills. Clouds now covered the sun, and a rain shower moved toward her. She quickened her step, but slowed as she neared the cabin door. The peas she and Will had planted were trying without much success to climb the log wall for the support they needed. *I need to find thin branches for them to have something to hang on to,* she thought as she rearranged a hopeful pea plant onto a nearby stake. *It is one thing I can do.*

She turned as the door opened, and a huge dog leaped toward her, knocking her to her knees. She heard Will's shout as she rolled onto her stomach to protect her body, while Will's shouts roiled over and around her. She felt his arms turning her onto her back, heard his voice whisper, "My darling, my darling."

Then everything went black.

When Florence opened her eyes, she saw the soft glow of evening twilight and the flicker of light from the fireplace coming through the thin blanket between their bedroom and the front room. She looked around to orient herself and bring back what had plunged her into darkness. She wiggled her toes; she lay on her bed with a warm brick wrapped in thick flannel tucked around her feet, and a light blanket covered her.

She lay still, trying to piece it together. Will . . . a strange dog slamming hard against her legs, knocking her to the ground. She seemed to remember hearing Will's voice and the feel of his arms lifting her.

"Will," she whispered. "Will . . ."

She closed her eyes, felt her fingers draw into a fist. Then he was beside her, his big hand taking her clenched hands in his. "I'm so sorry," he said, his voice a hoarse whisper.

"Will, what—what—happened? There was a dog—I don't understand."

She struggled to a sitting position, and Will slipped an arm around her, pulling her close. "Don't try to get up yet," he warned her. "I don't want you falling again."

"I don't think I will. Not with you beside me."

"Can you smile, Florence? Tell me you love me?"

"Of course I can. And I can kiss you, too. But not right now, I'm hungry." She eagerly sniffed the air. "I smell something cooking." A playful tone entered her voice, and the smile he waited for broke across her face. "What is it?"

"Potato chowder. I put in bacon and milk, butter, too. We can eat whenever you're ready."

She grabbed his arm and carefully got to her feet. "I'm all right, Will. Really I am."

"No aches or pains? No tender spots."

She shook her head. "Nothing. I—I just need to know. Did a black dog jump on me and knock me down, or did I imagine the whole thing?"

"He was real all right. But he's gone. When he jumped on you, I yelled, and he took off around the back of the cabin. I doubt he'll be back."

"But I don't understand. Where did he come from?"

"I don't understand it myself," Will said as he guided her to the table. "Does it really matter?"

He pulled out Florence's chair, and she sank into it. "Yes, it does," she said crisply and she heard irritation in each word she spoke.

"I bought him," Will replied.

Florence stared at her husband in shocked disbelief. "Bought him? What do you mean?"

Will picked up the bowls he had set on the table. "I'll dish up our soup, and then we can talk."

But Florence was more than just irritated. Emotions boiled up inside her and threatened to overflow. She bit her lips to hold them back.

"Would you like to say grace?" he asked as he set the steaming bowls in front of them.

"No," she said. She heard the anger in her voice, but she didn't try to stop it. "I'd rather hear you pray. Maybe you can ask God to be with the dog you brought home. Who knocked me down, then ran away."

Will gave her a long look, then bowed his head. His words were slow coming and shame rose up in Florence's heart. Tears pricked the back of her eyes, and she reached for Will's hand.

"I'm sorry, Lord," she whispered. "I feel bad, too. I know you said in Your Word to thank You for all things, so thank You for this wonderful chowder Will prepared. And thank You for the dog, too. Keep him safe and bring him back to our home. Amen."

She covered her mouth with her hand and fought back tears. "I'm sorry I acted the way I did. Please forgive me." She lifted a spoonful of chowder to her lips. "It's delicious, Will."

Their gazes met, and Florence saw weariness reflected in his blue eyes and the slight tremble of his lips. "I hate to say this, Florence, but I—I really did buy him. His name is Vaughn."

She stared at him incredulously. "You bought him? Without even . . ."

He nodded and laid his spoon beside his bowl. "It happened as I came around the corner by the saloon. You know, it's inside, in the back of the building there, don't you?"

She nodded and he continued his story. "Right out front near the hitching posts, a man—he was drunk, could hardly walk . . . Florence, he was beating his dog. I yelled at him to stop, but he wouldn't; he just screamed curses at me. Then I waved a bill at him and said I wanted to buy the dog. He nodded, grabbed the money, and stumbled across the street. I picked up the rope tied around the dog's neck and took off running down the road with the dog at my heels."

"How awful. Oh, Will . . ."

He turned to her. "He's been beaten before, Florence. He has a big scar on his back—the fur doesn't grow right there—and a split ear with part of it missing. I'm sorry about the money, but I had to do something—I had to."

"You did right," she said. "We need to pray he comes home. What did you say his name was?"

"Vaughn. I don't know where the name came from—I guess he just looked like a Vaughn."

Just then they heard something bump against the door, then a scratching noise.

Will and Florence looked at each other. The big, black dog named Vaughn had come home.

5

I know you have connections with us, Vaughn"—Florence reached out and touched the tip of his nose—"but we do have rules for you to follow. One of them is no begging at the table, the other . . ."

The pleading look in Vaughn's dark eyes as he cocked his head to listen grabbed at her heart. "The other is . . ."

The dog whined softly.

"You know what I'm talking about. It's one of the rules. No whining; your master said you're not allowed to whine, unless it's an emergency."

Vaughn brushed her hand with his nose and whined again. He looked longingly toward the door, then back to Florence who pushed her bowl aside and got up from the chair.

Vaughn followed, and the moment she opened the front door he was out. As he streaked around to the back of the cabin, she turned and sank into the rocking chair in the front room. Reaching for the hairbrush she had used earlier, she began to undo the dark braid down her back.

A quick knock, the front door popped open, and Aunt Amelia exploded into the room. "What's all this about a dog to scare away a mountain lion?" Her eyes blazed. "I call it a bunch of nonsense, is what I call it. In case you didn't know, we have enough problems around here without adding a puppy to the mix."

Florence laid her hairbrush into her lap and gestured toward the chair Will usually used on the rare occasions when they sat together in the front room. "Won't you please sit down, Aunt Amelia? Or would you rather sit in the kitchen? The tea-kettle is still hot, and we could have tea."

Aunt Amelia took a deep breath, slowly breathed out her mouth and deflated before Florence's eyes. "I'm sorry," she said softly. "I guess we could have tea. Is it warmer in the kitchen?"

"Yes." Florence smiled and held out her hand. "I love you, Aunt Amelia, and I don't want to make you unhappy. I have a story to tell you, the story Will told me about the dog who was abused right before his eyes. It happened yesterday."

Aunt Amelia nodded her head as she took Florence's arm. "I should have known there was more to it than I knew. I shouldn't have jumped on you when I came in."

"You already told me you were sorry. Now, let's have tea and we'll talk."

The tea cooled in the women's cups as Florence shared Will's story of how he came to acquire a full-grown dog. "I have to confess I was miffed when he brought home a wild dog that knocked me down when Will opened the door. Vaughn—Will named him—came from behind my husband and jumped on me. I lost my balance, then rolled onto my stomach. Then I fainted; it scared Will half to death."

"As well it should," Aunt Amelia asserted indignantly. "What did he do?"

"Will? He carried me inside and put me to bed. When I woke up, I found he'd brought in bricks wrapped in flannel for my feet. When I started to get up, he was right beside me, guiding me into the kitchen where he had a pot of chowder ready for our supper."

Florence shook her head and continued. "But I was still mad. It wasn't until he told me the dog had been beaten, it came together in my mind and in my heart. When it did, Vaughn scratched on the door; he's been here all night, and the big galoot is starting to love us already. You'll meet him in a bit. I just let him out a little while before you came."

But Aunt Amelia wouldn't let go of her concerns. "Tilly told me yesterday you've been sick in the morning. You know what it might mean, don't you?"

For a moment, Florence's hand covered her mouth in consternation. "Now, why did she go and say that?"

"She's worried about you, and so am I. You know what it sounds like, don't you?"

"I—I'm not sure."

"You will be soon. Have you been late on your monthly?"

"Only a little. But I've always been like that—one week, sometimes two. It doesn't really mean anything."

"But it might, Florence. You're married now, and things are different. I suggest you see Dr. Rutler, see what he has to say."

"A baby," Florence whispered. "I wonder what Will will say, if I really am pregnant."

"Same as most men I suppose. He'll get mad and then he'll get used to it. When the baby comes, he'll act like he did all the work. Proud as a peacock he'll be, you just wait."

There was a soft scratch on the door, and Florence went to check with Aunt Amelia behind her. She opened the door.

Vaughn stood on the steps grinning from ear to ear as only a dog can grin. "What do you think, Aunt Amelia? Is he smiling at us?"

"Yes, he is. Come in, Mr. Vaughn, and meet another member of the family," she invited. "My name is Miss Amelia and

I'm so glad you came. I only ask you to keep watch over my niece, especially when Will is gone. Do I have your promise?"

Vaughn stepped inside, sat down, and held out his paw. Aunt Amelia took it and shook it solemnly. She turned to Florence. "You know, I really think he knows what he's doing."

His reply was only a quick yip, but Aunt Amelia was satisfied. "I'm going home now. Remember what I said about Dr. Rutler," and she stepped out the door.

A lovely lady, Florence thought as the door closed behind her. *I wonder if Will and I really will be parents before the year ends.* Deep inside she knew she hoped her aunt was right. And then she wondered. What was Aunt Amelia talking about when she said we were having enough problems without adding a puppy to the mix?

It was the kind of question to keep one awake most of the night. Perhaps when Will came home, she'd ask him if he knew what Aunt Amelia was talking about.

But she didn't.

Florence wakened suddenly in what felt to be the middle of the night. She lay still in the darkness watching the varying shadows blanketing the room. Will's arm curled around her made her feel safe, but something bothered her, and she didn't know what it was. Her hand moved protectively to cradle her tummy. Tomorrow, Will would be at the store again, and she would be alone. Anything could happen.

Her thoughts raced. Men had to work to provide for their families. She couldn't expect Will to stay home when he had a job to do. *I wonder what he would think if I woke him to tell him we need to teach Vaughn to carry messages between the cabin and the tent? He'd probably say I was overreacting, and if he did, I'd have to agree.*

She closed her eyes to block the shadows and tried to pray. *Lord, You are my refuge and strength; my ever-present help in time of trouble. You know my anxious thoughts, and in the best way I know how, I give them to You.*

Except her thoughts wouldn't stop running. Slowly, carefully, she disengaged herself from Will's arm and rolled onto her side. Propping herself up on one hand, she fumbled for the matches she'd left on top of her open Bible and the candle she kept on the wooden fruit box that served as a stand next to the bed.

The match flared as she touched it to the wick. The soft circle of light calmed her, and she reached for her Bible and opened to the Psalms. *Be merciful unto me, O God, be merciful unto me: for my soul trusteth in thee: yea, in the shadow of thy wings will I make my refuge, until these calamities be overpast.*

She read it again, and then again, and each time she read it, her peace deepened. "Thank you, Lord," she whispered as she blew out the candle. "Now I can sleep."

She was only vaguely aware when Will bent over and kissed her lips. "I'm going to the store now," he whispered. "I love you, sweetheart. I'll be home at suppertime."

"Love you," she whispered, but heard only the soft closing of the front door. She turned onto her side and sank deeper into sleep.

When she wakened several hours later, sunlight streamed in from the east, pushing glowing fingertips of light into the bedroom. As she slid toward the edge of the bed to put on her stockings, the familiar nausea welled up into her throat. As she stood, she felt something wet splash down between her legs.

She lifted her gown, saw a puddle of blood between her feet, and screamed. At the same moment, Vaughn streaked into the room. He sniffed her hands and the puddle beneath her as she sank back onto the bed. But she was in the shadow of God's wings, wasn't she? *Lord, I've made you my refuge. Show me what to do.*

Her hand went out and touched the silky fur on Vaughn's head. "Sit, Vaughn," she said, and he sat. She leaned forward. "Amelia," she said it slowly, distinctly. "Remember Amelia?"

Vaughn licked her hand as though he didn't quite understand. "Aunt Amelia—go—to the tent. Find Aunt Amelia and bring her home. Now." She bent down and smeared her fingers into the blood on the floor, then on the white spot beneath Vaughn's chin. She reached for her cane and almost fell. *Have mercy on me, O Lord, have mercy.*

She stumbled to the door and opened it, and Vaughn leaped past her. She stared after him as he disappeared down the path to the tent. Leaving the door ajar, she returned to her bed, lay down, and closed her eyes. The words she'd read in the night whispered through her being. *Yea, in the shadow of thy wings will I make my refuge, until these calamities be overpast.*

⌘

Aunt Amelia took charge the moment she stepped into Florence's room. She cleaned the floor, gathered up clean towels from the kitchen to use for a padding beneath her, then brought in a cup of lukewarm tea. "It's the best I can do," she said. "The good thing is you're not bleeding now. But you're probably a bit dehydrated, and you must start drinking water, lots of it. And stay flat. I'm going for the doctor."

"But, Aunt Amelia," Florence protested, "Wilsonville's too far and you . . ."

"I'm old. I know. But . . . I'm going to the neighbors first. If someone from there can go for Dr. Rutler, I'll be back shortly."

She stood looking down at her, and Florence read love and concern in her dark eyes. Before Aunt Amelia left, she brought her tea and a glass of water and kissed her on the forehead. "Stay brave," she said. "Remember you're not alone. Our Lord is with you. And Vaughn." She turned to the dog that stood just inside the room. "You take good care of my girl," she said. "You hear?"

Then she was gone. Florence heard the door close behind her.

"Will," she whispered, "I wish you were here." She took a deep breath and took a sip of the warm tea, then followed it up with the water. Vaughn poked his nose onto the edge of the bed, and her fingers lingered as they traced the outline of his nose and cheeks. "Thank you for saving me," she whispered. For a moment, her gaze lingered on her Bible. "We just have to trust God and wait."

But she didn't have to wait long, at least not for Aunt Amelia to return. As soon as she ascertained Florence was no worse, she headed for the kitchen. "I'm making up the fire first," she announced. "Then you can have something hot. A cup of chamomile tea would do the both of us a world of good."

"Did you find John? Is he going for the doctor?" Florence asked.

"I didn't go to the Moads, I went to the Murray's instead. They're closer, and there aren't steep places to climb once you get past our canyon. They're nice folks, and the old lady's about my age, I'd say, maybe a bit older. She sent me down to the barn where her son was cleanin' out the stalls. He's a nice fellow. Kind of glad for a break, I think. Anyways, he saddled up and took off at a fine gait. I sort of expect Dr. Rutler here in an hour or so."

Aunt Amelia did more than fix tea. She took the beans Florence had put to soak at the back of the stove, added bits of

bacon and chopped onion, and soon had a hearty soup bubbling. It wasn't even done when Florence heard Will's voice in
the front room. "I came right away," he said. "Where's Florence?
Is she all right? Is Dr. Rutler here?"

"She's in bed and needs to stay flat until the doctor arrives.
He'll tell us what to do. In the meantime, she'll tell you what
happened."

"The roses are gone from your cheeks," Will said as he
dropped to his knees beside the bed and cupped Florence's
face in his hands. "What happened, honey? I need to know."

Florence's lips twisted, and sudden tears flooded her eyes.
"There was blood when I stood up," she wailed. "Lots of it. I
didn't understand what was happening, and it frightened me.
If I hadn't had Vaughn, I don't know what I would have done."

"Vaughn? I don't understand."

"I don't either. But he knew what to do when I rubbed some
of the blood on the white spot on his neck and told him to go
get Aunt Amelia. He brought her back, and she went to the
neighbors to see if they could send for Dr. Rutler."

Vaughn let out a low woof. "I think he's here now," Will
said. He took his bandana from his pocket and gently wiped
the tears from her face, then smoothed back the dark strands
of hair that escaped her braid.

Dr. Rutler stepped inside and Will turned. "Would you like
me to ask her aunt to come in?"

"Yes, please. Sounds like I need to check this gal of yours
out, and I think she might feel better with another woman
present." He set his black satchel on the floor beside her and
sat down on the edge of the bed. "Now, what's been going on
Mrs. Will?"

Florence told him everything, the nausea she'd felt the past
few weeks, the lateness of her monthly, and then the gush of

blood Amelia had cleaned up before he'd come. "It scared me," she whispered. "It just didn't feel right somehow."

"And it wasn't, my dear." He turned to Aunt Amelia as she came in and stood by the bed. "Florence says you cleaned up the blood. Was there any tissue in it? Anything didn't look quite right?"

"No," her aunt replied. "I checked the padding and the sheet, too. It was only blood."

"I'm going to do an examination now. Breathe slowly, Florence. It'll be over in a short while."

When it was over, he went to the kitchen to wash up, then asked Will to join them as he explained his findings.

Will brought in a chair for Aunt Amelia, and the men sat down on the edge of the bed. "She has all the signs of early pregnancy. However, it wasn't a miscarriage; there's no evidence that the baby was expelled. Two things are possible, and only time will tell.

"If the baby has separated itself from her, it won't survive and will come later. However, it may be the baby is still attached. And you"—he nodded at Florence—"will feel life as the baby begins to move." He smiled and gently patted the back of her hand. "But it won't be for some time. Either way, your nausea and discomfort in the morning may continue; it's hard to say."

"Will I be able to get up?" she asked. "Resume my daily tasks?"

"I'd like for you to stay flat for the next forty-eight hours. Then you can have meals with your husband. But stick to quiet tasks like sewing and reading until the bleeding stops completely. Most of the time when this happens to an expectant mother, the bleeding gradually stops after two or three weeks. But even then, you need to take it slow. No heavy tasks like gardening or mopping and sweeping. Above all, don't do any heavy lifting. Leave it for the girls to do; they can be here in a few minutes."

He gestured toward the window, then got to his feet. "Sounds like they're home from school now. May I tell them what happened, Florence? Or would you rather?"

Florence shook her head. "I think it would be good if you told them. They love you dearly, and there's such a special bond between the three of you."

Even as she spoke, the door opened and both girls rushed inside. "You'll never guess what happened to us on the way home!" Tilly exclaimed. "We saw a man lurking in the trees by the bridge. He looked like one of the horse thieves who stole our Callie last year!"

"We think it could have been the awful thief who lassoed our Callie," Faye cried. "He's the one with freckles on the back of his hands, and I'm scared of him."

"It was close to the place where they stole her," Tilly added. "We spotted him right where we turn off on the curvy road. Even though he was in the shadows, he looked to be—skulking in the bushes. In other words, he seemed to be trying hard not to be seen. It could be the horse thieves are back and searching for pack horses like before."

But Will shook his head. "Seems a bit odd to me. Since they finished the railroad over the pass, they aren't using horses to pack in supplies."

"Mightn't they need horses, though?" Dr. Rutler asked. "Surely they're still being used in the distant mines. Why, I bet there's still gold coming out of those Klondike hills and rivers. I think we owe it to each other to keep a sharp eye on our horses and mules and pass the word around, too."

Will nodded and Dr. Rutler beckoned to the girls. "Let's go outside. I have something I want to tell the two of you."

The girls nodded, and the three of them went out into the sunshine.

6

A June breeze stole softly across the porch where Florence sat in the chair Will had built for her.

He's like me, she mused. *He enjoys communicating his love for the ones he loves by making them something special with his own hands. Something they'll enjoy. Tilly's the same way.* She smiled. *And if it has to do with food, there's Aunt Amelia.*

She slid both hands back and forth over the maple arms of the chair, savoring their smooth surface and the intricate designs caught in the golden wood. Over time, the patina would subtly deepen, enhancing its beauty much like the eastern sky now sending its pink and gold morning glory onto the tops of the trees.

Soon the sun's face would smile through the giant firs and flood the freshly sawed boards on the floor of the porch Will was constructing. "I'm building it for you," he'd said. "Since you can't wander around like you used to, for a while you need a place outside where you can enjoy summer's coming, even if you're cabin-bound."

But it's for Tilly and Clarence, too, she thought. *They'll need the added space for their coming wedding, and they've been so good to us.* She shook her head, remembering the long winter evenings and days Tilly had spent with needle and thread as she adjusted the puffed sleeves of her wedding dress to perfection. Now in less than a week Tilly would wear the dress as she stood beside her groom. Together they would pledge their love.

For a moment, tears threatened to overwhelm her, but she pushed them aside. Even though they'd all expected the two would wed, they hadn't expected it to be so soon. Tilly's one desire was to have an outdoor wedding at the cabin beneath the trees. When Will suggested they have it on the porch instead, they were elated.

Although the porch was still unfinished and without a roof, Will had found a stand of young firs in the grove near the giant tree whose shape reminded her and Tilly of a sitting bear who bounced when the high winds blew. Will felled one of the firs, then cut it into lengths to support the roof of the new porch extension. Together he and Callie with the help of their neighbor had pulled them one by one through the woods and across the field to the cabin where they now lay in the side yard.

"They won't be the lovely white pillars of your dreams, honey," he said, "but they will be pillars, rustic pillars. And they're ours, our very own, harvested with my own hands from our land."

She caught a movement out of the corner of her eye, heard a soft step on the porch edge, and turned. Tilly stood, Vaughn beside her, gray eyes smiling at her. "We surprised you, didn't we?"

Vaughn rushed to Florence and laid his big, black head in her lap. "Good morning, Vaughn." Her slender fingers moved to his head as she gently smoothed back the fur between his ears. "This is a surprise. Did you miss me?"

She looked up and caught Tilly's smile. "Talk about a two-family dog and soon to be three. Oh, Tilly I'm going to miss you and Faye."

"We'll miss you, too," Tilly said. She looked around, a faint frown crinkling her forehead. "You need another chair out here. Do you care if I get one?"

"Not at all. It would be nice to have more sitting space. I could even serve coffee and tea and enjoy family and friends sometime. Dr. Rutler says it's okay for me to walk around now, you know. Even outside—but to take it easy. In other words, pamper myself."

"And your little one," Tilly whispered. "Oh, Florence, is it really going to happen?"

"We don't know yet, but the good doctor thinks there's a good chance the baby's still alive and growing. We won't know for sure until I feel life, and it won't happen for a couple of months."

"I don't see how you do it. When I think it could happen to me by next year even, I get goose bumps. Just think, we might have two little ones close enough to grow up together."

"It's all I could ever dream and more," Florence confessed. "To think a baby I might give birth to will one day call me Mother awes me. It's hard to comprehend. To me it's more than we can ask or even think about, as Paul writes in Ephesians 3 where he talks about God's power."

"But God," Tilly mused, "there's nothing too hard for God. I mean, Mary was a virgin, yet she gave birth to the baby Jesus. We just need to trust Him."

Florence nodded. "Most of the time I do. But sometimes in the night, with the darkness all around, doubts come."

"I understand," Tilly exclaimed. "I mean when Daddy left to find gold and we were so alone." Her eyes turned smoky with emotion. "I wonder sometimes. Will I ever see him again? The

Klondike is so far away. And we haven't ever received a letter from him. I'd give just about anything if he could be at my wedding."

She gestured toward the end of the porch as she continued. "Clarence and the parson will be waiting for me there when I step out the cabin door dressed in our wedding gown." She frowned and bit her lip. "Do I trust God? Yes. But it doesn't mean Dad will come home. I have to learn to trust God, even if He says no, for reasons I can't understand."

Vaughn laid his big head in Florence's lap, and she looked down, absently caressing his ears. "I think it takes a lifetime to really learn what it means to trust God. These past weeks I've had time to read a lot. Most of the time it's been in the Psalms, where God keeps reminding me He's my Refuge, my Rock and Shelter, a very present help in time of trouble. And then there's the verse in Hebrews 13 that says He'll never leave us or forsake us."

She looked up and was surprised to see tears streaming down Tilly's cheeks. "But, Tilly," she cried, "it can't get any better, can it?"

"No, and that's the whole idea: It just can't get any better because when we come to Him, He gives us everything we need to live a godly life." Tilly grabbed up a handkerchief tucked in the pocket of her faded denim dress and wiped her eyes. "Florence, I'm sorry you had to stay down so much these past few weeks, but oh, those verses God laid on your heart met the need in mine. Thank you, my friend, my sister. They were exactly what I needed."

Then Tilly was gone. Florence and Vaughn watched her run down the steps, then disappear down the path that led to the tent. Soon would come the wedding; then this time a man and a woman in bridal attire walking hand-in-hand toward a shack to call home high on the bank of the Willamette River on the other side of the settlement.

⌒

The morning of Tilly and Clarence's wedding, Florence wakened at dawn's first light with a feeling of well-being such as she hadn't felt in a long time. Could it be the verses she'd shared with Tilly earlier had brought such peace?

She whispered the words again like harbingers of peace. "God is my refuge and shelter—He will never ever leave me, and I am safe."

She reached over and touched Will's pillow, still warm from the indentation of his head and whispered, "I love you, Will."

A sudden shadow darkened the open doorway, and she caught her breath. Will had come into the room and now stood beside the bed. "You don't have to whisper you love me, sweetheart," he said as he sat down on the edge of the bed. "As far as I'm concerned, it's something you can shout to the world!"

"Even to the sun?" She smiled as she touched his cheek with her fingertips. "Were yesterday's clouds blown away by the wind in the night?"

"Not quite, but they're on their way. We'll know more come dawn. It's on its way and so is our breakfast." He leaned forward and gently kissed her lips. "The coffee is fresh and hot, and I can whip up a skillet of bacon along with the eggs Tilly brought. What do you think?"

"I should be up and doing breakfast. I might not be able to manage the sweeping and mopping, but I can manage breakfast, especially with you right there to help with things I'm not supposed to do."

Fifteen minutes later, wearing a simple gray dress, she tended a tin platter heaped with bacon and fried potatoes at the back of the stove while she stirred eggs and milk together and poured them into the hot skillet. It gave her pleasure to set a cup of hot coffee in front of her husband, then plant a kiss on the top of his head.

"You're feeling better this morning," he said as he playfully grabbed her hand.

She smiled, snatched up a potholder, picked up the platter of hot food, placed it in the middle of the table, and sank into the chair beside Will. "I'm so glad Clarence scythed the field. You know, the place we sometimes call The Green. It's even more beautiful now—just perfect for a wedding."

Without another word, they bowed their heads and silently gave thanks to the One who had brought them together and provided for their needs. While they ate, they discussed the wedding to be held in the afternoon on the porch.

"Although they're planning a simple wedding, it will be lovely. When Tilly tried on my wedding dress, it brought tears to my eyes," Florence confessed. "She added a couple of tucks at the waist and, since she's a bit shorter than I, turned up the hem a couple of inches and basted it in place. You can't even see the stitches."

"A couple of women from the church are bringing over a wagon full of roses from their yards, and one of the men from there built an arbor the couple can stand under while they repeat their vows," Will said. "Clarence told me they're also bringing benches for the people to sit on, seeing as we don't have many chairs. I expect they'll be here early."

It happened just as they planned. As the yard filled with horses and a rustic assortment of buggies and wagons, the kitchen came alive with baked potatoes bursting their skins, a variety of fragrant breads and vegetables, casseroles, and a leg of lamb that dominated the stovetop. Florence, standing by the table dressed in her ivory silk blouse with its tiny embroidered pink rosebuds, counted the pies and cakes on the sideboard over which Will had placed a large plank to make room for the extra food.

Then it was time for the wedding. The morning sun stood high in the sky, and the aroma of fresh cut grass and roses filled the air as the men slid the wooden trellis mounted on flat lengths of lumber onto the north end of the porch. The women swarmed around it with their roses and fastened the blooms with the longest stems near the top.

While they carefully arranged buckets filled with garden flowers along each side, Florence slipped into the bedroom, clutching the pearl necklace in her hand. Tilly, her tawny hair brushed until it glowed gold, stood in her white dress peering into the mirror. She turned toward Florence and opened her hand to reveal a cluster of dainty white roses.

"Aunt Amelia and Faye brought these for me to wear, except I don't quite know what to do with them." She held it up to her neck. "What do you think?"

"It needs to be in your hair, the pearls at your neck."

"But I'm not one of the family," Tilly protested. "You're expecting and I have a feeling it's a girl. She's the one who needs to wear them on her wedding day."

"Nonsense. You and Faye—and if indeed I do give birth to a daughter—I'd like each of you to wear the pearls on the day you're wed. You both are daughters of my heart. I can't help but feel my mother would be overjoyed if you wore the necklace today, if for no other reason than to remind us of the love between our families. Love stretches and grows; the golden cord cannot be broken."

Florence hugged the girl then took the brush from her hand. Gathering up the locks on the sides of her face, she fastened them together with a comb to which she attached the tiny white roses. "And now the pearls," she murmured as she fastened the clasp at the back of Tilly's tanned neck.

Tilly's mirror face almost crumpled, then she whirled and threw both arms around her friend. "You better go out and get seated," Florence whispered. "I think I heard the flute."

The trill of music accompanied her as she drifted to the front room where Will waited. He took her arm and escorted her onto the porch down to the rose-covered trellis where a chair awaited her. She sat with Will standing behind her and looked around. The guests had made themselves comfortable, most on the porch benches, a few of the younger ones with small children sitting on the grass when the flutist began to play. The notes soared over the crowd and to the tops of the trees. It echoed across the canyon and brought a lump to Florence's throat when the parson, followed by Clarence, stood in front of the trellis.

The bride stepped forward as the wedding march swelled through the sweet tones of the flute. Tilly stopped in front of the reverend, and he held out his hand, placing her hand into the strong fingers of her beloved Clarence. A crow cawed, a squirrel scolded, and then a deep hush fell over the crowd.

The reverend spoke into the waiting silence. "Inasmuch as we are gathered together in the sight of God . . ."

A feeling of loss coupled with fear swept through Florence. They were so young, so inexperienced. Were they ready for the difficulties ahead?

Words came from somewhere deep within her soul. She knew they were from her Lord. *I am their Refuge, their Rock and Shelter, a very present help in time of trouble. I will never, ever leave them or forsake them.*

In the best way she knew how, she bowed her head and gave the young couple into the hands of her Lord.

7

Florence stood on the porch looking out at the morning. High above her head the upper branches of the mighty old-growth firs flirted with the high winds. Their soughing wakened longings deep within her. The woods, the garden, called to her; if only she could feel the flutter of life deep within her womb, know beyond a shadow of doubt her baby was healthy and growing.

It's almost the end of June, she thought. *I need to walk at least to the top of the canyon or even into the garden. But I promised Will—Dr. Rutler, too.*

She looked down as Vaughn danced a circle around her, saw gladness leap into the dog's eyes as she stepped to the edge of the porch. She dropped to one knee and drew his head into her arms. A blue jay dipped over the cabin roof, then settled into the fir on the north end of the porch where Clarence and Tilly had stood and pledged their love, promising each other to love, honor, and obey until death parted them.

An unseen squirrel high in the branches broke into a flurry of indignation. She turned her head and spotted him craning his neck to look at her from behind the trunk of the tree, his comical face creased with anxiety. "Are you telling me I have to stay here and wait for Will to come home? What are you saying?" she asked.

She laughed aloud as the squirrel popped out of sight, then reappeared, his stiff fluffy tail arched indignantly, his worried chatter filling the air. Vaughn woofed a low note of warning; the squirrel disappeared again, then reappeared as he scampered upward to the heights spitting out his concern to anyone who would listen.

Florence smiled and shook her head. Not yet the garden, not yet the canyon below, yet they still beckoned. "Come on, Vaughn," she said, "let's go back inside."

But instead of moving, she stood still and lifted her face to the sky, rejoicing in its blueness and the wispy scattered clouds tumbled by the wind. "Lord," she whispered, "I promised Will and Dr. Rutler I wouldn't walk alone outside. But most of all I promised my baby, and You know I'd do everything I could to give my child every chance. Please give me a quiet spirit while I wait, and in the meantime obey You in all things."

She opened her eyes, and when she did, she saw a sudden movement in the alder grove at the top of the canyon. A deer? A mountain lion? No, it wasn't an animal. Someone, a man in faded blue clothing appeared to be watching her from behind the tangled brush.

Cold fear clenched her stomach. Tilly and Faye had seen a man lurking in the trees by the bridge only a few weeks ago and thought him to be one of the horse thieves who had come through the previous year looking for horses to sell to prospectors who needed pack animals to get their supplies over the pass. But Will said it wasn't probable now, as the newly constructed railroad near Skagway had done away with the need for horses to pack into the Klondike.

But was Will right? She took a deep breath. What should she do?

Vaughn must have noticed the man as an intruder, for the dog leaped off the porch and launched across The Green toward the canyon. She shouted his name, but he didn't seem to hear as he continued at breakneck speed toward the thicket where she'd caught a glimpse of the stranger.

"Vaughn, come back! Come back!"

Vaughn skidded to an abrupt halt and turned. He changed direction, then like an arrow let loose from a bow he headed straight for her. As he neared the porch, she reached over the edge to grab his collar.

The dog stopped abruptly, jerked backward as Florence fell face forward off the porch edge and onto the grass. Vaughn whined and nosed the back of her head as though trying to help, but when she tried to turn over nausea welled up inside her.

She forgot the lurking stranger and shouted. "Help! Please! Someone help me!"

There was no reply, only the soft sound of a bumblebee as it flew close to her nose seeking the nectar of the white clover struggling to survive in the thick grass.

———

In the evening the lowering sun winked through the firs, casting their long shadows over the cabin while Florence, stretched out on the bed, told Will about it. "I'm not sure how long I lay there before I heard footsteps. At first, I didn't connect him with the stranger I'd spotted earlier in the bushes. To me, he was simply a gentleman who heard my cry and came to help."

"What did he say?" Will asked. "More importantly, what did he do?"

"He rolled me onto my back, then scooped me up in his arms. His hands were gentle, like a woman's. He carried me to the bed and brought me a glass of water, even sponged my face and asked me where I hurt.

"I told him about our baby and how much we wanted to have our little one. I even told him Dr. Rutler didn't want me to wander outside on the uneven ground, because he was afraid I might fall and he wasn't yet sure our baby was safe. Then the man volunteered to go into the settlement and find the doctor."

"Very kind of him. What did you say?"

"I said I thought I was okay, but then I felt uncomfortable giving him either my name or yours." Florence sighed. "I don't understand it, Will, perhaps because I suddenly remembered the stranger I'd glimpsed before I fell. Maybe he wasn't someone I should trust—not a friend at all, perhaps even a horse thief. But even thieves can be kind to a woman in distress. At least, it's what ran through my mind."

She sat up suddenly. "Remember last spring when the girls saw someone skulking near the bridge where the curvy road dips down and then up as it curves toward our road? They were almost sure he was connected to the horse thieves who came through last year stealing our horses, mules, and donkey to sell as pack horses in Skagway. But he didn't have freckles on the back of his hands like Tilly described." Her lips tightened. "And Tilly did say the man who took our Callie was a big man resembling one of the thieves she'd seen before."

"When you went to their camp with Hal, before you moved into the tent, you didn't recognize the stranger who helped you as one of them, did you?"

"No, I can't say I did. But I felt a prick of caution when he asked me my husband's name. He said he was looking for a Mr. Nickerson, sometimes called Nick or Nicky, but I just shook my head and told him I was Florence. Then I pretended to be hurting and made a funny face to distract him. After all, it wasn't any of his business, was it?"

"No—but I wonder now what his business was. Why was he lurking in the bushes watching the cabin? It doesn't make sense. You don't just wander off a trail when you're on someone's property."

"Maybe he didn't care," Florence said softly. "But then, maybe he did. When I look back now, I think I let fear rule me when I yelled the way I did. I feared for our baby—afraid to move because I might do something to hurt our little one. I think I was operating on fear, not trust. I'm sorry, Will—about my poor judgment—at least it's how I feel about it now. Will you forgive me?"

"There's nothing to forgive, Florence. Really there isn't. You were scared and hurt and I wasn't here."

Florence reached up an exploring fingertip and touched the hairs curling backward in his eyebrow. "I love you, Will," she whispered. "So kind you are and wise, too. I'm so glad you married me."

"And I'm glad you married me. Glad you followed me to my tent and loved me enough to patiently wait for me to return from the far North." He put his arms around her and pulled her into his arms. "I'd still feel better if Dr. Rutler were here."

Even as Will spoke the sound of a horse's hooves clattered to a stop out front. Dr. Rutler's rousing "Whoa boy. Whoa now" penetrated the walls of the cabin.

"We'll have to pay him well for coming all this way with only the word of a stranger," Florence said. They grinned at each other.

Will went to the door and shouted a greeting to the good doctor. Although Florence didn't quite hear what they said, the men's obvious concern reached out to her.

When the two came into the bedroom, her stomach tightened. "Am I really all right?" she asked and was surprised to hear sudden fear coloring her voice.

Dr. Rutler put a reassuring hand on her shoulder. "I just have a few questions and then a surprise. Your Aunt Amelia and Faye have been cooking, and they're bringing dinner over in a while. I daresay a good hot meal is just the medicine you need."

"But how did you know Aunt Amelia was planning our supper?" She shook her head. "Somehow the pieces aren't quite fitting together, Dr. Rutler."

"They aren't, are they? But let me hear your version first." He sat down on the edge of the bed and leaned forward, listening intently, as she told him about her fall and the stranger who came when she called.

"He carried me inside," she confided. "Did he find you at the settlement? Ask you to come?"

"Yes, he did. He seemed to be a good man. He told me he was from Seattle and had met the sheriff in charge of an investigation into a gang involved in sheltering stolen horses destined for Canada. Evidently, his own brother had also been involved in the state of Washington and lost his life. When his body was found in a nearby ravine in early spring without a cent on it, a Nick Nickerson from our area, who had been his brother's partner, became a suspect and the sheriff was looking for him."

Florence shook her head as fresh fear flooded through her, catching her breath and making it difficult for her to swallow. "Did he say why he thought so? Does he think this Nick is an alias for Will? More importantly, does Will know?"

A sheriff in Seattle. Dr. Rutler had said the man who had come to her aid was looking for a man was suspected of being an accomplice of the one who had helped his brother with the horses and then stolen his cash wages. But Will would never have done such a thing!

What now, she wondered. She fought tears as she reached and traced the edges of the Tree of Life quilt the ladies of the church had given them on their wedding day. Somehow just thinking about the women who carefully cut, then stitched the squares together reminded her of their love. Her imagination took wing; might each stitch be someone's prayer winging its way to the Father in heaven? Not just for her but Will, too?

The conviction grew deep within her thoughts given her by the Holy Spirit. *I'd like to do one from the same pattern,* she thought. *Make it our very own.*

Only the color scheme would be different. She pictured a quilt touched with silken embroidery in yellow to set off the green. But what if her hands stiffened with the coming of winter? If God answered her and Will's prayers the way they longed for Him to do, it would mean a newborn baby to care for. Would she find time to stitch a quilt?

"Lord," she whispered, "Dr. Rutler was glad for my answers to his questions the night after I fell. When he examined me, he said he's pretty sure the baby's growing and the fall I took off the porch hadn't hurt anything. But he also said the restrictions must remain, since we wouldn't know for sure until the flow stops and I actually feel life."

Life, new life. Outside the front room window, a robin had built her nest. Half hidden in a lower branch of the rapidly growing sapling at the south end, the nest escaped detection until Florence had spotted it earlier in the week by the sudden winged activities of the parents of the newly hatched babies.

She watched as the mother swooped into her nest with a worm dangling from her beak. *Food for the little ones,* she thought. *She doesn't have hands, but she gets the job done.* She spread her own fingers and looked at them carefully. The kitchen work she'd been doing was helping her regain agility in her fingers. She felt it whenever she cut the small radishes to mix with the lettuce for their evening meal and when she peeled and sliced, then mashed the cooked potatoes into whipped peaks of melting goodness.

Suddenly, she remembered a piece of flannel she had placed in the bottom of the rag bag in the kitchen. A soft yellow piece of fabric, sprinkled with tiny blue birds, that she hadn't quite known what to do with. She smiled. Too pretty for dishrags or even a kitchen towel, it would be perfect for a gown for their baby. Making a gown from the remnant could be her act of faith to lift the burden she and Will carried and ease their worried hearts.

When Will arrived home, he found her sitting on their settee carefully stitching the pieces of flannel together that she had cut from a pattern she carried in her head. She held it up eagerly for him to see.

"Do you like it?" she asked.

He took the soft pieces and examined them carefully with rough calloused fingers toughened by long hours of outdoor work. Those hands had sawed, hammered, and labored in the garden with first the plow and then the hoe, and now . . . When he lifted his head and looked at her, she saw tears edged his lashes—one slowly slid down his tanned cheek.

"What does it say to you, Darling?" she whispered.

"I need to have faith. To believe, to trust God has power to make miracles happen, even in spite of our weakness. Our baby . . . Then I start thinking we'll never have a little one to call our own—ever." He reached up his hand and wiped his tears onto his sleeve. "And now He's given you the faith to believe, to use your hands to create a special gown for our little one. You don't know what comfort it brings, Florence."

He put his arms around her and drew her close. Together they sat while the lowering sun peeked in and then out of sight behind the shadowy firs. As dusk descended around them and deepened, so did the silence, and Florence sensed the petals of wild honeysuckle opening, as if whispering messages of hope.

Soon, blossoming stars would meet the departing sun's last blaze of light only to be embraced by the air as it took on a violet tinge. The birds had madly chorused during the day and now chirped in a desultory fashion as they settled to roost among the tree branches or perhaps settle into their nests.

As Florence drew away from Will's arms, she saw he slept. She almost wanted to slip out the door and watch the night darkness fall around the cabin, to be there for the stars as they slowly appeared like pinpricks in the darkness. Instead, she tiptoed into the kitchen and lit the kerosene lamp. She stirred up a fire in the stove and put on a kettle of water to boil. What would they have for a light supper? Perhaps cold biscuits smeared with the freshly churned butter Will had brought home from Hal's store and the applesauce Aunt Amelia had canned in the fall. There was also a plate with a couple of pieces of salt pork stowed in the wire cupboard next to the kitchen. She brought it in, plopped the meat into a cast-iron skillet, and added in some leftover beans. Then she decided to remove the stove lid to set the pan directly on top of the flames. She did the same with the kettle, then reached for the plates and utensils.

She made the table attractive as she spread a fresh tablecloth and centered a woodsy bouquet of pink clover and ferns Aunt Amelia had brought earlier in the week. She looked up and smiled a welcome as Will came in and sat down at the table.

"Something smells wonderful," he said.

She gave the beans and pork a quick stir. "We'll have to wait until the kettle boils for our tea."

She opened the jar of applesauce and placed it on the table alongside the cold biscuits. "If I'd had my wits about me, I would have put them on the stovetop to warm."

"No problem. I'm not exactly particular about food, you know, as long as it's plentiful." He reached over and grabbed her hand. "But you, Florence, you are my star. Having you as my wife and now a little one to join our family is almost too much joy to comprehend."

He pulled her close and kissed her. "What do you think about choosing a name now even though we may not know for sure it will happen? I think doing so would strengthen our faith. What will we name her if she's a girl?"

"Amelia Anne is pretty, but so is Elizabeth Anne. What do you think?"

"They're both winners. Do I get to pick a boy's name?"

Florence nodded. "We can always change it if we want to. What's your favorite boy's name?"

"I've always favored Lester. It's such a manly name, strong, upright, trustworthy, too. Surely we can find a middle name to fit with it."

"Like William maybe?" A sudden impish smile flashed across her face. "We can call him Will for short."

"They used to tease me with it, volunteer me for everything. 'Will will do it. Will will.' Will will dish up our beans, too. They're starting to smoke!"

He jumped up and grabbed a potholder. In what seemed like one quick motion, he pulled the skillet off the stove and pushed the stove lid into place.

He brought the pan over to the table and filled their plates. And all the while, grinning from ear to ear.

"You say grace," he said. "Please."

Florence nodded and bowed her head. "Thank you, Father God, for giving me a husband who is a man of faith and courage. Thank You that he loves me even though I almost burnt up our supper."

Their eyes met across the table, the dark brown and the blue. "A blue-eyed girl for me, a brown-eyed boy for you," he said.

Florence smiled. The three of them were safe in God's hands, and what could be better? Both of them together, in their own way, faced their future in faith and confidence. They would trust their God, no matter what.

8

Florence woke as light from the sun pushed its way into the room. Daybreak had come, but Will was gone; she knew it even before she touched his empty pillow. She pushed back the covers and quickly arose. Her feet were bare; her night-gown swirled around her ankles as she headed for the kitchen.

The stove and teakettle were warm to the touch; the coals in the wood box glowed red. She dropped in kindling and a couple of pieces of wood knowing that even though she didn't feel hungry, she needed to eat for the sake of their baby.

Just remembering the sweet moments she and Will had shared the evening before brought tears to her eyes. Disappointment, too. Somehow, she'd fully expected they'd have breakfast together, but instead she'd overslept and missed her opportunity to spend time with the man she loved. Will being the kind of man he was would never have wakened her to fix his breakfast. Perhaps, she thought, he's spent too many years on his own.

"But he loves me now," she whispered as she reached for the oatmeal. But would it be enough? She'd been strong and healthy when they'd first met. She remembered the fun they had together exploring First Street in Portland, the hours they'd spent rummaging through the stores and peeking into fancy restaurants to see how the rich people lived. And always they were laughing together, enjoying each other.

Then came the stormy night when she found out he had spent all his money to purchase a desolate farm without a house, only a tent in the forest, and she'd been so devastated she refused his ring. If it hadn't been for Aunt Amelia, she knew she would never have had the courage to follow him and await his return from the distant gold fields of the Klondike, where men fully expected to find their fortunes in a pile of gold. Even though he might return empty handed, she knew she wanted the man she loved, no matter what.

She still wanted him.

"I wish I could be one of those women who pop out a baby every year or so, do all their own work, and sometimes help in the fields," she whispered to the silent kitchen. "They also feed the hungry and help care for the sick. It's what I want to do—except I can't."

Her voice rose higher and she was almost shouting. "It's not fair. It's not fair at all! So there!"

She heard a soft step and whirled around to come face to face with her Aunt Amelia. "Are you having a fit?" the older woman demanded. "What will the neighbors think?"

Florence stared at her aunt, feeling young and suddenly very foolish. "You—you are the neighbors," she said weakly. She stumbled to a chair and sat down abruptly. "I'm sorry, Aunt Amelia. I've—I've been worried, is all. Will and I—" She buried her face in her hands and burst into tears.

Aunt Amelia stepped forward, encircling her with both arms. "There, there, my dear," she soothed. "A lover's quarrel perhaps? We've all had them, I'm sure. But it's not good for you to get all upset like this, especially not for the little one. You haven't had breakfast yet, have you?"

"No. But I don't know if I really want anything." Florence covered her nose with the back of her hand. "May I please borrow your hankie? I'm still in my nightgown."

"I can see that," Aunt Amelia said drily. She reached into her pocket and handed her a handkerchief folded into a neat square. "Go ahead, wipe your eyes and nose. You can keep it if you want. Now you just sit there while I stir up the fire a bit. It's high time you ate something, is what I'm thinking. Afterward, we'll talk."

But they didn't. The stack of golden brown pancakes covered with butter and boiled brown-sugar syrup brought comfort as did the scrambled eggs laced with tiny bits of salt pork and fresh parsley. Aunt Amelia called Faye and Vaughn, as they played chase the stick together on The Green, to join them for breakfast. They came eagerly with Vaughn, who showed his appreciation for his mistress by stopping to lick Florence's hand and looking up at her with a doggy smile.

"You're the best cook ever, Aunt Amelia," the small girl explained after breakfast, "the very best."

But it was Faye's words addressed to Florence that reached her soul. She whispered into Florence's ear as she followed Aunt Amelia out the door. "I saw the baby gown. It looks a little bit like a love song."

Florence stared after the child. The child's words spoke truth to her soul. She had something to give; already her stitches were her love song for her baby. Perhaps one day her song might even communicate love to another generation. *Oh, Lord, let it be.*

The next week took on a totally different flavor. Although Florence had managed to be up and about when Will left in the mornings, he'd told her straight out he preferred getting his own breakfast and he felt better when he left if she still rested in her bed. Although she always had a hot meal waiting for him in the evenings, he seldom arrived before dark, and then he was so tired and cranky that he sometimes almost fell asleep over his plate. Florence missed the sweet camaraderie they had shared earlier. Sometimes she wondered what he was doing in the settlement to take so much of his time. Surely he couldn't be working at the feed store all those hours. After all, he'd only been hired for part-time work.

"I feel like I'm fermenting all the time lately," she told her big, black dog friend. He lay stretched out close to her feet as she sat at the table, a hot cup of tea before her. "Sort of like a bubbling yeast jar set too close to the stove. I wish I knew what to do."

Her companion whined softly, his dark eyes fixed soulfully on her face. "You miss him, too, don't you?" She continued, "Sometimes I feel he won't come home and I'll be sitting and waiting all alone until morning. And then when I seek him out, I'll find he's gone and left me all alone like he did when he left for the gold mines of the Klondike."

Vaughn leaped to his feet, leaned against her knees to lick her hand, as though trying to reassure her she'd never be left alone. He'd always be there for her.

She hastened to explain, "Oh, Vaughn, I could get along without him, as long as I had you." But even as she said the words aloud, she wondered if she could. The trips to the spring for water with no Tilly to help, harvesting the garden with only Aunt Amelia. Why, just finding enough wood to keep the fire going would be difficult. Then adding in the care of a baby and laundry. There'd be lots more laundry then. Would she really be able to do it all?

She shuddered and pressed her cheek against Vaughn's face. When she did, she heard a hesitant knock on the door. Vaughn made a low "wroof" sound, trying to be a low-throated, deep growl as he headed for the door with Florence close behind.

She recognized Trapper Gus through the window and gladness shot through her being. She flung the door open and an instant later was in her old friend's arms.

"Well, well, well," the old man exclaimed as he clumsily patted her back. "Just thought I'd stop and see how you folks were a doin'. Heard young Tilly up and got herself hitched to the city feller with the red hair. Ain't it somethin', now?"

Vaughn pawed at her visitor's feet, who absently fingered the dog's ears. Florence stepped back, took his hand, and drew him inside. "I'm so glad to see you!" she exclaimed. "As for Tilly and Clarence, we think they're perfect together. Have you been to the tent?"

"Nope. Just saw the smoke and figured you and your Will must have tied the knot and live over here now. Seems like I heard somethin' about it, though."

Florence nodded. "The neighbors got together and raised the cabin in a day. It was wonderful. We had to wait for the windows to come on the steamboat."

She invited him into the kitchen followed by a clatter of doggy paws. Once there, she glanced around, glad she had taken time to wash the dishes and wipe down the table. However, Gus would not care, of course. She had a feeling his little cabin was probably filled to the brim with trapper paraphernalia and animal skins she couldn't even begin to imagine. Besides, bachelors were known for their tumbled surroundings. And one as old as Gus . . . She smiled and shook her head. Surely, he'd be the king of an untidy domain.

Gus glanced appreciatively around the room. "It's pretty in here what with all the sunshine comin' through the window.

You're not goin' to up and make curtains and shut it out, now, are you?"

She shook her head. "If I do, I'll only make narrow ones to frame them. You'll see. I won't spoil anything."

Gus bobbed his head up and down several times. "I like it," he said. "Now, how about me goin' out and fetchin' you some wood? You're goin' to need some for your next meal."

"Why, Gus, it would be wonderful. I remember the first time we met. Remember how Tilly brought you a hatchet and you said you'd rather use an ax?"

"No, can't say I do. But I shore do 'member the meal. Your Aunt Amelia's biscuits just about melted in my mouth. If I rustle up the fire, would you fix me some?"

"I sure will. It will be my pleasure."

As she lifted a bowl from the shelf and took out lard, baking powder, and flour, she realized her worries had quieted. Where was the yeast? Ah, there it was. She was glad someone had moved the jar away from the hot stove. It was likely Trapper Gus, short for Gustafson, had done for her what she'd been too distracted to do for herself.

A nameless tune bubbled up from within her. It felt good to have an old friend fire up the stove while she mixed up a batch of flaky biscuits for him. Now if they'd just turn out as good as Aunt Amelia's, she would be satisfied.

A thunderstorm pushing its way up the valley in the early hours before dawn on Independence Day startled Florence awake with a loud clap to shake the window and set her upright.

"Will," she whispered.

For a brief moment her hand cupped his jaw, but he slept on. Lightning illuminated the room, and she saw the wall hanging and rough logs almost as clearly as day. Another thunderclap and she swung her legs over the bed's edge and hurried to the open window.

Another lightning flash and the swinging fir branches were etched in light. She heard a branch hit the edge of the cabin in the brief lull before the thunder rumbled again, growling out its warning.

She jumped as an arm slipped around her waist.

"Are you all right?" Will asked.

She nodded. "I had to get up and watch the storm. Seems to me Independence Day is putting on her own celebration—except it's a bit early."

They both caught their breath as another clap, a moment of silence, then a loud crash from somewhere in the canyon shook the cabin. Will's arm tightened around her. "Sounds like one of the firs went down. Don't be afraid, Florence."

"But they're so tall and we're so small. Almost I wish we were somewhere in the middle of a field where nothing could reach us."

"Except a bolt of lightning could hit us. Standing in a field would be the worst place to be. I'll take my chances in here under the trees."

"We both will. I—I'm so glad you're here beside me, Will. Sometimes I feel so—so all alone." She looked down not wanting him to see the tears gathering in her eyes. "How about us going into the front room so we can look out over the canyon?"

"Good idea." He took her arm and guided her, even though she knew she could have easily found her way. Another lightning flash and once again the picture it created stayed in her mind's eye as clear as day.

Will drew up two chairs in front of the window. Gradually contentment and a quietness descended over Florence's spirit as they sat together with hands linked watching the storm.

"I won't be going into town today," Will said suddenly. "Is there anything special I can do to make today a day to remember?"

Florence giggled. "Nothing we can do could ever compete with this display. I know it's something I'll never forget."

"Nor I. And the best part of all is sitting here with you while God lets loose His thunder and lightning. See what I mean?" he said as another flash lit up the meadow spread out in front of them.

"I wonder if a tree went down," she mused. "If it did, I hope it didn't do too much damage."

Will tried to reassure her. "Nothing much it could hurt, Honey. It's all forest."

He doesn't even think about the growing things caught in its path, she mused. *Nor the animals living there.*

They watched in silence as the lightning strikes became less brilliant, the thunder rumbles more distant as a curtain of rain advanced across The Green. The end of the thundering celebration was fast approaching, but it had been everything she could ever imagine, and more.

When Will pulled her to her feet, she was glad. "Let's get you back in bed," he said. "Morning will come before either of us is ready."

Will was right, except when the morning sun rose and spread its warmth over a wet world, he was ready. A fire in the kitchen stove welcomed Florence, as did her husband who took her hands in his and drew her to the table. She sat down and inhaled the fragrant aroma of coffee.

"You look beautiful, all dressed and ready for the day," he said. "Do you always put on an apron when you first get up in the morning?"

"Why don't you stick around a bit longer in the mornings? If you did, you wouldn't have to ask." The moment the words were out, she knew she'd said the wrong thing. "I'm sorry, Will. I shouldn't have said that."

"Maybe not, but you're right, Florence. We haven't been able to be together a lot these past few weeks. But things happen. Sometimes you're prepared, sometimes you're not."

He poured a cup of coffee and set it on the table, then sat down with his own cupped in his hands. "There will be a time soon when I'm going to have to leave you for a little while. I don't know when, or how long I'll be gone, but it will be soon."

He put his cup on the table and reached for her hand. "I'm sorry, Florence. I left you before without a word of explanation when I went off to the Klondike. I won't do it again ever, I promise."

"But why, Will? I mean our baby. I—I need you." She covered her face with her hands, and her voice came out muffled in her own ears. "So does our little Elizabeth or Amelia. Our baby Lester. Don't we—I mean they—mean anything to you?"

"They and you mean everything to me, Florence. It's why I have to go. I don't know when exactly. But I promise you now, I will return before our baby is born."

He got up abruptly and headed for the door. But not before Florence saw his dear face, crumbled and broken with a lone tear sliding down his cheek.

9

In the afternoon, Will moved the table out onto the porch. "We can pretend we're having a picnic," he explained. "I'd take it out onto the grass, but it's too wet. Too easy to slip and fall."

Florence agreed with him. In spite of the rocky start to their morning, they had been able to set their concerns aside and concentrate instead on enjoying their day. Will had brought home a small beef roast that Florence coated with flour, dusted with salt and pepper, then seared in hot grease to hold in the juices while it baked.

Later in the morning, Will brought in tiny carrots and potatoes along with green onions with their tops still intact. "Why, those onions are the size of a walnut!" Florence exclaimed. "Aren't they a bit oversized?"

"Doesn't matter. My mother used to lay onions like these over the top of the meat about halfway through baking," he said. "Then she put the carrots and potatoes all around the edge till the pot was chock-full and then some. Then she made gravy before she served it. It was delicious."

Florence brought out her best tablecloth with the water lily embroidery. She'd stitched it with her own hands when she lived with her brother and his wife in their proud Victorian house overlooking the town and the river. *That same river flows less than two miles away,* she thought. *I could never have dreamed then I'd be living upriver in a cabin in the woods, married, and expecting a baby.*

She unfolded the cloth slowly over the table. She remembered how Opal had sent it with her brother on her wedding day. Inside was a note saying she wanted Florence to have the tablecloth so she could use it after she married. Today, they'd use it for the first time.

She went back into the kitchen, took out a cookie sheet to use as a tray and loaded it with napkins, utensils, plates, and glasses that she brought out to the porch. Will stood beside the table and watched her set each piece in its place before asking her if there was anything he could do to help.

"Yes, please." She pushed back a lock of her dark hair that persisted in getting in her way. "We need a bouquet to make our celebration meal perfect. Could you fix us one?"

For a moment, Will's face was a study in consternation. "But—but what would I use? A bouquet? We don't have flowers in our garden."

"Someday we will," Florence assured him. "Today we need a bouquet. A wild one would be perfect, or even one from the garden. If worse comes to worse, just poke a few fern fronds into a canning jar. We have lots of those."

"Which ones, ferns or jars?"

"Both," she replied. "Just get something green if you have to, but pay close attention, you just might spot a flower. Surely, there's something in bloom out there."

"Any particular spot?"

"Just out and about. I guarantee you'll find something growing somewhere. Surprise me, okay?"

A tenderness she hadn't felt in a long time nearly overwhelmed her as she watched him cross The Green, then disappear into the canyon. He didn't know what he was doing; he didn't like it, but he did it for her because he loved her. End of story.

When he returned, his arms were loaded with frothy white oceanspray and furry pink blooms she'd once identified as steeplebush. "It's all I could find," he said as he handed her his armload of flowers.

"Why, you have enough here to celebrate ten Independence Days!" she exclaimed. "Now, if we can just find enough containers."

In the end, they filled six quart jars with the delightful arrangements. "One for the table, two on each side of the door leading into the cabin. We have enough for both ends of the fireplace, another for the stand beside our bed. Oh, Will, it's just perfect."

Their dinner was perfect, too; the roast meat almost melted in their mouths, and the vegetables were fork-tender. Even the dark, rich gravy served over the meat and potatoes was delectable.

Will groaned as he pushed back his empty plate. "Talk about perfection. I couldn't eat another bite if I had to."

"Nor could I." Florence leaned back in her chair and closed her eyes. She stirred as the sound of a horse and buggy came up from the canyon. "I think we're about to have company, Will."

Will nodded. "Sounds like John's buggy. I wonder if he needs something."

Except it wasn't John, it was Martha. She met them on the porch carrying a covered cake pan. "I got carried away with my baking yesterday," she said as she set the cake on the table. "It's for your dessert. Later, of course—the cake is bursting with rich chocolate flavor. You'll probably be able to enjoy it this evening."

Will thanked her for coming and then excused himself. "I have a feeling he might be going to take a nap," Florence said as she watched him go inside. "He's been working such long hours. Having a farm to take care of and a job at the feed store has pretty much worn him out."

Martha pushed back the strands of her graying hair creeping out of the bun fastened on top of her head. She turned to Florence and impulsively hugged her. "I should have come much sooner. I'm not exactly sure now why I didn't. But today . . ." She shook her head. "It's why I baked an extra cake. I couldn't get you out of my mind. I decided right then and there, I was going to bring it to you. Besides, things are rather quiet at our house."

"No grown children to come home to Mom and Dad?"

Martha shook her head. "God never chose to bless John and me with children of our own." She smiled at Florence, her cloud-gray eyes serene. "Perhaps it's why I so enjoy my youthful neighbors. Tilly, especially, and little Faye have become dear to us. And you and Will, too. Having you wed in our home meant a lot to us. I just don't see you as much as I do the young ones."

Martha pulled out a chair and sank into it. She leaned forward and took Florence's hands into her own. "Tilly was in church on Sunday, and when I asked how you were, she said you've been feeling poorly lately. Is it the rheumatism again?"

Florence shook her head, and to her consternation, her throat tightened. For a moment, she sat clinging tightly to her friend's hands. "My fingers are still stiff, but they're so much better. I've even started to do a bit of sewing—for our baby— except we don't know yet whether it's really going to happen."

"Oh, child, I'm so sorry, so very sorry." She reached into her pocket and pulled out a folded handkerchief. "This one's for you; I always carry two. One never knows when one might need an extra."

Florence wiped her cheeks and blew her nose, then continued. "Dr. Rutler says I may have miscarried in the spring, but he's not sure. It's why he's doesn't want me doing any heavy work. Will doesn't want me walking around outside either, he's so afraid I'll overdo—or trip and fall."

"I'm glad you have the porch, you need the fresh air."

"I know. Dr. Rutler says I'll feel the baby move soon if it's still alive and growing. Except, I honestly wonder whether or not I'd recognize it for the real thing. Seems like it might be easy to mistake it for something else."

"I know what you mean," Martha said thoughtfully. "But I remember my niece telling me it was different somehow; it feels more like the soft flutter of butterfly wings."

Florence gazed out at The Green below. Even as she watched, a Monarch lit on a clover blossom, its orange and black wings moving with the clover's gentle sway. She lifted her hand and the butterfly moved toward her. Almost she could touch its fluttering wings.

She covered her lips to hide their sudden quiver, then jumped to her feet. "Are you ready for some lemonade and a piece of your wonderful cake? I am."

—◦∞◦—

The next few weeks picked up speed, and time almost seemed to fly. Will said the brothers didn't need him at the store, so he spent his days on the farm with Faye tagging his every move. They became a fixture—the tall, serious man in overalls and a favorite red and plaid shirt, the little girl in a loose-fitting pinafore followed by the black kitten who had grown under her tender care into the mighty Blue, as she often called him.

Since the chickens had been roosting high in the trees behind the cabin, Will decided to move the shed nearer to the cabin. After a day of taking it down piece by piece and carrying them to the new site, they tackled the complicated job of putting it back up. Clarence drove his horse and wagon over, filled with extra boards left over from his own barn-building project.

The two men worked through the afternoon as Aunt Amelia took over dinner preparation in the cabin kitchen while she fussed over the new project.

"In the end it will be a blessing," Florence countered. "You and Faye won't be spending another winter at the tent, and you know it. Besides we need extra room to store hay for Callie and baby goat. We already have the hay Will scythed earlier. He piled it up underneath the big fir at the edge of the flat until he could get back to it."

Just saying the words made a longing rush through Florence. What she wouldn't give to be able to see the canyon in all its summer glory, to follow a deer trail through the woods, then stop to wander into an intimate glade sheltering wild strawberries and the crawling vines of the small-leafed forest blackberries.

The afternoon sun was warmer now, but the cabin lay swathed in the shade of the giant firs at the back of the cabin. Their shadows now covered the porch and invited her outside. She picked up the diaper she had cut from the white flannel Martha had brought and took it with her to the porch where a chair awaited her.

Faye sat in the grass nearby with Blue enthroned upon her lap watching the men hammer and saw. As soon as she spotted Florence, Faye dumped her cat into the grass and dashed over to where Florence sat. "I like coming here," she said. "It's starting to feel like home."

"But you'll soon be back in your old home high above the river. You sort of miss it, don't you?"

"I don't know. I don't remember. But if I want to go to school with the rest of my class, I have to be at Tilly and Clarence's. Clarence is making us a big barn, and Tilly says she made new curtains to make the shack pretty."

"You'll miss Aunt Amelia, though, won't you?"

She nodded. "But most of all, I'll miss my Uncle Will. You don't care if I call him that, do you?"

"Of course not. He's a good uncle."

"I'd call you Aunt Florence 'cept you seem too young to be an aunt."

"Aunts don't have to be young, they just need to be nice."

"You are nice, but he's more fun," she said and jumped off the porch. She lit on The Green on her bottom, scrabbled to her feet, then ran to join the men, with the ties on her pinafore loose and flying after her. Florence shook her head. So much for the hours she'd spent teaching Faye to make daisy chains. Or the dandelion ladies with the long curls they created by stripping the stems into tendrils to show off the beauty of their golden petal skirts.

She paused suddenly. She recognized the sounds of Hal's wagon before she saw it, and sure enough, he was coming up from the canyon, waving his whip and shouting at his horses. Two large barrels in the back bumped against the sides of the wagon as he pulled the horses to a halt.

He waved his hat at Florence and shouted, "Brought you the barrels your man ordered! Is he around somewhere close by?"

Even as he yelled, Will and Clarence came up alongside the wagon, and together the three men worked the barrels off the cart and onto the ground. "We can roll them to where you want now," Hal said.

Aunt Amelia came to the door, a big spoon in one hand and a mixing bowl balanced against her other arm. "Just put them in the front near the door, right up under the eaves where they'll catch the rain water in the winter time," she instructed. "We had one of those at the school where I last taught. Came in mighty handy."

She started to turn and go back inside but stopped. "You want to stay and have dinner, Hal? It's going to be quite early, but we have to get an early start tomorrow, what with Will here and my Faye havin' to get up at the crack of dawn to help Will plant those late taters they're talkin' 'bout."

Hal inclined his head and doffed his hat in Aunt Amelia's direction. "Many thanks for the invite, but my Irene always has something fixed so the three of us can eat together afore little Maud's bedtime. 'It's family time,' she says, 'we have to preserve it no matter what.' So I best be gettin' back."

Hal's words sparked a feeling of desolation deep within Florence, but she held her head high and pasted on a courageous smile as he strode by the front of the porch. "Give my greetings to Irene," she called.

He turned and grinned at her. "I sure will, Florence. She talks about you a lot, misses your visits to the store."

"I miss them, too," she said. "But with Will helping out at the feed store, getting him to pick up what we need is a cinch."

"Mighty convenient if you ask me." He lifted his hat and waved as he climbed up into the wagon. "Giddap, Polson. You too, May. Time to get movin', our little Maud's a-waitin'."

The horses plunged down the hill, and Hal and the wagon disappeared from sight. Florence bowed her head. *Our little one is a-waitin' too. But, Lord, sometimes my faith is so weak.*

She felt a hand touch her shoulder and looked up to find Will smiling down at her. "You look like a young Madonna sitting there with a diaper in your lap and your arms cupped beneath your tummy. You're a beautiful woman, Florence. I'm proud to call you my own."

"But you didn't come here just to tell me that, now, did you? Be honest."

"You know me too well, my dear wife. Hal sort of jumped the gun when he brought the barrels I ordered. Actually, I planned to bring them myself as a surprise."

"I don't understand, Will. How would you have brought them here, great big barrels like that? It doesn't make sense."

"Clarence and I are building a wagon for Callie," he explained, "one to match the size of the barrels. This way you and Aunt Amelia will have an easier way of getting water to the cabin. All you'll have to do is hitch Callie to the wagon and go down to the creek, use the buckets to fill the barrels with water, then haul them back."

Sudden understanding rushed through her. "Why, Will, all we'd do then is guide Callie under the eaves and unhitch her. It's a wonderful idea!"

"Just be patient a little longer." He slid both arms around her and she leaned into him, snuggling close to his chest. "Clarence and I still have a bit of work before we can finish the project. But it won't be long, I promise."

"And you always keep your promises," she whispered. "Will, I know I can count on you."

Afterward though, she thought about the words she'd spoken. If she counted on Will, a mere man to keep his promises, why then did she have so much trouble trusting God?

Florence woke suddenly. One moment she'd been wading in a sun-drenched pool with a butterfly fanning its wings on the back of her hand, the next she was lying in her bed staring down at bright quilt blocks making a craggy mountain peak over her feet.

A veil of peace spread over her—butterflies, a pool, clear water. She reached over and touched her husband's cheek, felt the faint stubble of whiskers beneath her fingertips. She studied his face in the faint light of early dawn. Her Will, how dear he was, her husband forever.

She took a deep breath and relaxed. A soft flutter like a butterfly's wings deep within her womb. She lay as still as she could. Another flutter, whispers of hope from their baby, from their God. She sat up and shook Will awake.

"Our baby!" she cried. "It lives!"

He was awake in a moment, his arms cradling her while he moved an exploring hand over the soft skin of her stomach. "I don't feel anything," he said. "Are you sure?"

"Yes, yes, I'm sure, Will. It was just like Martha said, 'the soft flutter of a butterfly's wings.' Will, we don't have to be afraid any longer."

"Our child lives."

10

Weeds in the scraggly uncut grass of the neglected Green stood knee-high as heat from the August sun sapped their energy and zest for growing. Although some were still green, most had shriveled and dropped their seeds in preparation for the coming winter. In other areas, where the grass had been repeatedly trampled, dry soil showed through.

Florence smiled as Will walked across toward the porch where she sat stripping plump beans from their pods. "Just a few more days in the sunshine and they'll be just right to put away for winter." She flicked a bean with her thumb and finger and sent a firm, fat one flying his direction.

Will snagged it out of the air with one hand held high. His arms and face were brown as a chestnut, but his hair shone light brown, flashing gold whenever a sunbeam found it. His eyes were as blue as the color of the sky behind him, and she loved watching the play of green and blue mingled with glints of gold as the light changed in them. It felt good to her spirit to see he'd put the restlessness and darkness he'd carried since late spring aside, even if only for a day.

"Are you ready for a pot of beans?" she asked. "I could sink one into the coals of the fire pit in the backyard. With just the right amount of the maple wood you cut up, it would hold fire all night and be ready for tomorrow."

"If you fix up a pot, I'll see to the fire." He put his hands on the porch's edge and vaulted up beside her. "What'd you think of my catch?"

"I'm impressed. Why, you'd have been pitching a baseball if you'd been anywhere else besides our little settlement."

Vaughn whined softly, and Will squatted onto his heels and gently smoothed the worried frown forming between the dog's eyes. "Don't worry, boy. I don't need a baseball or a bat, not when I have you."

"And me," Florence added.

They smiled at each other, the sweet camaraderie Florence had feared they had lost forever sparking between them. *If only it would stay this time*, she thought. *If only* . . .

Will laid his hands on her shoulder. "I love you, Florence. Will you always remember it—no matter what happens?"

"I—I don't know what you're trying to say, Will. Is there something you're not telling me?"

He sighed. "Just—some things I ran into in Seattle may need my attention. Remember the man who helped you when you fell off the porch?"

"Yes, I do. He was kind, but somehow I feared him."

She licked her lips then asked the question she feared to ask. "Did he ever get a chance to talk to you, Will?"

He reached for an empty chair, drew it forward, and seated himself across from her. "Yes, briefly. He came into the feed store."

"What did he say?"

"He'd be coming back through soon. If he does, I may need to return to Seattle."

"But why? It doesn't make sense."

"Misunderstandings and judgment calls don't always make sense, Florence. But nonetheless if it's something with power to hurt someone, I may need to do something."

"Even something you're not responsible for?"

Will sighed. "I can't tell you the whole story, Florence. Actually I don't know the whole story, at least not yet. Right now, I need you to trust me—even if I have to leave you for a little while."

Sudden fear knotted Florence's stomach into a hard knot. She took a deep breath. "Our baby," she whispered. "You—you said you'd be here when it was born. You promised."

"And I'll keep my promise, too, Florence. I will."

"No matter what?"

He nodded. "No matter what, Sweetheart, I'm going to be there for you. Just trust me."

"You said it before," she whispered. "If you go, will you tell me? I mean—I don't think I could bear to wake up some morning, or in the middle of the night, and find you gone without a word. It would break my heart." She jumped to her feet and collapsed into his lap.

"I promise, my darling."

Their lips met and their tears mingled as they wept together.

An unidentified sound startled Florence awake. She sat up. Will was gone, first light seeped into the room, and a breeze from the open window touched her bare arms.

She shivered. And then she heard it—a light scratching sound at the front door. Vaughn—Vaughn was gone, and Will—where was he?

Apprehension wrapped around her as she slid out of bed and scurried to the front door. The scratching noise came again. She opened the door, and Vaughn exploded into the room, dancing around and around her in an ecstasy of joy.

"Oh, Vaughn! Where's Will? Where is he?" But even as she cried out, she remembered Will's words, *I'm asking you to trust me—even if I have to leave for a little while.* Afterward, he'd held her tight while they'd cried in each other arms.

She dropped to her knees beside the dog and gathered him into her arms. He licked her face, and a soft whining sound came from somewhere deep within him. *Like soul meeting soul, and we both want the same man,* she thought. But Will had said he wouldn't leave without telling her first, hadn't he?

Perhaps he simply couldn't sleep and went out to get some fresh air. She swept back into her room and snatched up the light wrap she'd left at the foot of the bed. Sliding her arms into the garment's sleeves, she thought she heard the faint crackle of paper. Her searching fingers found the pocket and she reached inside. The feel of crisp paper twisted her stomach into a knot as she drew it out.

She leaned close and tried to read the words, but could barely make out the writing in the dim light. She reached for a match, struck it, then touched its golden flame to the candle. Will's words leaped out at her. She read them aloud as Vaughn nestled his head upon her knees and looked soulfully into her face:

> *My darling, darling wife,*
> *I wanted to wake you and tell you I was leaving. But I hate good-byes. If I had to say it aloud, I would never have left, I love you that much. Instead, I took the coward's way out and am trying to keep the promise I made to you that if I left, I'd tell you. Hold on to this note until you receive a letter. This is my promise to write as soon as I can.*
> *XOXO*
> *Your loving husband, Will*

Tears welled up in her eyes as she traced the circles for hugs, the big Xs for kisses, then laid the note beside the candle and leaned forward, gently rubbing her dear Vaughn behind his floppy black ears. "You don't like it, do you?" she whispered. "I know you miss him, and I'm so sorry. It—it's almost like opening a book and finding the character in a brand new chapter and not knowing how he or she got there. But this is worse, so much worse. Oh, Vaughn, are we going make it without him? Our baby and me—you, too."

She tried to smile through her tears and was rewarded by a loud thump from her furry friend's tail. She closed her eyes, and a prayer without words ascended from her heart to the heart of her God.

She even heard His answer deep within her soul. *I will never leave you or forsake you. You are mine.*

"Don't leave my Will either, Lord," she whispered. "Put a hedge of protection around him and keep him safe for me—and for our baby—and we mustn't forget our Vaughn."

Florence stood in front of the kitchen stove still dressed in nightgown and wrapper trying to coax a flame from the smoldering fire. She blew softly, and the slumbering coals caught flame from the kindling she had laid inside the firebox. She waited a few minutes, then added a couple of larger pieces of wood and closed the door. She'd soon have hot water for coffee.

She went back into her room and dressed quickly. She chose the red gingham apron Aunt Amelia had given her at Christmas to cover her serviceable gray dress and slipped it over her head.

Sweet memory, she mused as she tied the apron into place, but beautiful nonetheless. God had answered her prayer for Will's safe return from Skagway on Christmas morning. Surely He could do it again. *Except it needs to be before Christmas this time. Please, God.*

Back in the kitchen, she noted the slow steam rising from the kettle spout and got out the pot she used for brewing coffee. She heard a soft knock and poked her head around the corner.

"You've got visitors," Aunt Amelia called.

"Come on in," Florence invited.

The door opened wide, a delighted Vaughn danced in front of the older woman, then pawed at Faye, who had come in behind her aunt. The seven-year-old grabbed his upraised paw and solemnly shook it. "Yes, Sir," she said. "Yes, Sir, Mr. Vaughn. Aunt Amelia did bring her famous rolls. And yes, there's one for you, but we have to say grace first. Do you understand?"

"He understands all right," Aunt Amelia exclaimed as she set the covered tray on the table. "But he's not gonna get anything from me, I promise."

Florence pursed her lips to keep back a smile. "Well now, he might just be smarter than you think," she said softly. "What's bothering you, Aunt Amelia?"

"I guess I'm kinda mad at the good doctor. He thinks I should move into town."

"Why, what did he say?"

"He said I needed to move into town so I wouldn't be so isolated out here in the sticks, and he wanted to see more of me. Why, he even had the audacity to show me a small house a little ways past the school. But I told him no way was I gonna move off the farm. Why, you're most all the family I have left, and I don't like towns. Besides, it won't be so long before you present me with a newborn nephew or niece. I want to be here to celebrate with you."

"But you have Faye, and you adore her."

Her voice softened with emotion. "Yes, I do. It's almost like she's my own young'un, but come this fall she'll be living with her sister. My place is here and I know it."

"I agree with you, Aunt Amelia. And—and right now I need you." The tears she had bravely held back suddenly overwhelmed her, and she started to cry.

With one quick movement, her aunt took her in her arms. "Will's gone," Florence wailed. "Some legal thing in Seattle he needs to take care of. He seems to think he'll be there awhile, and I—I'll be all alone, except for Vaughn and the chickens."

"And Callie and Baby Goat. And don't forget the chickens now, or Faye's Blue. 'Cept she'll probably take him with her when she leaves."

Florence took a handkerchief from her apron pocket and wiped her nose. She lifted her head. "Someone's coming." She ran to the front door and looked out. "It's Dr. Rutler!"

He slowed his horse as he drew closer, then pulled to a stop beside the new hitching post Will had put near the porch only a few days earlier. For a moment, Florence's thoughts overwhelmed her. So many things Will had done to make it easier for her before he had to leave. The little wagon he'd made for her and Callie, and then the simple lean-to he'd built onto the horse and goat shed to house the wagon were ready for her use, whenever she might need supplies from the settlement.

As Dr. Rutler stepped inside, she flew into his arms. "Your man is gone," he said as he patted her back. "But you're not alone. You got us here to help you out, and help you we will."

"Hugs help," she whispered. She drew back so she looked into his face. "Aunt Amelia is here too. And"—she lowered her voice—"I smell cinnamon rolls."

She heard the shrill whistle of the teakettle and smiled. "Come on in. Make yourself at home, and we'll have coffee."

"Is it gonna be enough?" Aunt Amelia worried. "How about I cook up some oatmeal mush? It always sticks to a man's bones."

Faye chimed in. "A little girl's, too, but I like the rolls best. Can't we have both?"

"But, of course, we can," Florence said. She looked at their eager faces and knew she had her God to thank for their being there for her when she needed them most.

"I'd like to take a look at the wagon Will built and the lean-to as well," the good doctor said suddenly. "Sounds to me like he's quite handy with a saw and hammer. His gift could come in mighty handy in these parts. Would you care if I went out and had a look at what he's been doing?"

"I'll go with you," Florence volunteered. "If Aunt Amelia doesn't need my help."

"Oh, go on," her aunt encouraged. "Faye and I will do just fine without you. I'll send her out to call you when it's ready."

"Walking is good for you and the baby," Dr. Rutler said. "Try to do some every day now. It will keep you from getting depressed—something pregnancy often causes."

Florence nodded. "I felt pretty awful those early months when I couldn't do much of anything. But I feel better now since I've been able to be up and about. And Will and I, we had some special times together." Her voice caught. "I just wish he didn't feel he had to leave."

"It's a tough situation. Did you know he was going to stop in to see me before he boarded the boat?"

She shook her head. "No, we didn't talk. When I woke up he was gone, but he left a note, promising he'd be back by the time our baby was born. Did he tell you his reason for leaving?"

"What did he say to you, Florence? Since you're his wife, you really ought to know."

Florence sighed. "He told me he might need to return to Seattle to take care of some unfinished business, but I kept thinking he wouldn't have to. But he did . . . It's about all I know, Dr. Rutler. If you can help me better understand, I really need to hear it. It seems as though I do better when I deal with reality, rather than what my wild imagination has power to conjure up."

"I think you have something there, all right. I guess it's pretty much true for most women." He put an encouraging hand on her shoulder. "We men have a hard time telling the women we love our weaknesses and failures. Most of all our stupidity. To his credit, Will wanted you to know; he just didn't know how to tell you, partly because what he knew was pretty sketchy, but Will being the kind of man he is felt you needed to know at least as much as he did."

"And what was it . . . ?"

"Will was thought to have been involved in a horse-stealing operation when he hired on to bring horses to a remote ranch in the outback. They were to be kept there until they could be shipped over the border into Canada. It leaked out to the authorities that he had stolen those horses to enable his cohorts to ship them to the Klondike when the ice and snow broke up, and they could get through to the Klondike to sell them to miners there. Evidently it was a big money operation, but it wouldn't be the prospectors who'd come home rich."

"But Will wouldn't do it!" Florence cried. "He's an honorable man, and he doesn't think like that at all. It's just not my husband!"

"You know it and I know it, but they don't. It's why I'm here today."

"Was it the man who came when I fell off the porch? Was he the one who was looking for Will?"

"I'm not sure. Will said he was the brother of the man he had worked with on the Seattle wharves loading and unloading the cargo ships. I understand he looked Will up to warn him the authorities were looking for him. The two men talked and decided to go up to Seattle together after he finished some business in Portland.

"Both the brother and Will felt he could prove his innocence if he could find the man who had worked with him to move the herds and who had the papers signed by the owner to prove they'd been hired to bring the horses to some remote ranch to winter over. The problem he faced was his friend had left and given Will his share of the money they'd earned, to keep for him while he went into town for a shave and a haircut. But he never came back, and Will couldn't find him anywhere."

"But what if he doesn't find him? What if . . ."

"Don't go there, Florence, it's not something you need to do. Will is doing what he thinks is right to clear his good name. He needs you to be behind him, praying for him, believing in him, and letting him go."

"He's already gone, and I didn't have anything to do with it, not really." She lifted her chin. "But I know God is with us both. We just have to trust. We have to believe." Her voice broke as a sob rose in her throat.

Dr. Rutler finished her words for her. "And then you have to wait. But you're not alone. We wait with you."

He waved toward the cabin where Faye stood on the porch waving them in with both hands. "Breakfast is ready!" she shouted. "Please come!"

As they crowded into the kitchen, the smell of fresh coffee and cinnamon flooded their senses. Faye reached out and grabbed Dr. Rutler's hand in one hand, Florence's in the other. "We're going to say grace now, and I'm going to do it.

"Dear Father God, we thank You for all You do for us and all You're going to do. We love You and trust You and thank You for these beautiful cinnamon rolls and Aunt Amelia who baked them for us. In Jesus's name, amen. Let's eat."

And they did. Only Florence saw Faye smuggle a cinnamon roll under the table where Vaughn lay quietly at her feet. He took it like the gentleman he was, and when Florence caught the little girl's eye, she winked.

Faye winked back and Florence smiled. *Will,* her thoughts whispered, *I wish you were here to enjoy it with us. But our day will come. God will bring you home in His own time. All we have to do is wait.*

11

Florence stood at the kitchen table looking out at the September morning that heralded an early fall. Already a killing frost had swept over the area leaving gardens bleak and blackened. Pumpkins and squash vines sprawled useless on the dirt, and bean vines clinging to their poles sagged listlessly.

The night before, an unexpected cold front had moved through the valley bringing a chilly rain to further dampen Florence's spirit. It lingered a few days, then left. At night, a hard frost transformed their world into silver, gray, and black.

"It's too soon," she whispered to Vaughn who lay happily at her feet chewing contentedly on an old bone clasped between his front paws.

She looked at the biscuit dough on the flour-coated table in front of her. She gave it a quick roll, picked it up, and whacked it hard against the palm of her hand. Even as she did it, she felt the little one leap in her womb, and her spirits lifted.

She glanced up as Aunt Amelia came into the kitchen shaking her head and making tsking sounds with her tongue. "You treat baking powder biscuit dough like that for very long and you're gonna have biscuits mighty hard to eat," her aunt warned. "Could even break a tooth."

Florence stood still, her hands overflowing with dough. Heat rushed into her cheeks. "I'm sorry, Aunt Amelia. I guess I forgot."

"Probably got to dreaming and forgot it wasn't yeast bread. I've done it myself a time or two." She stepped over to the stove and held her hands out over its warmth. "I'm glad you have a fire started. It's chilly out."

"Chilly? It's almost like winter. It's raining hard again, and it's a cold rain. I don't like it much."

"Nor do I, but 'tis life. So much left to be done, what with potatoes and turnips needin' to be dug and squash and pumpkins ready for the root cellar."

"I haven't received any word yet from Will, either." Florence laid the dough on the table and gently began patting it to ready it for cutting into squares. "I hope biscuit dough is as forgiving as you are, Aunt Amelia."

Her aunt laid the sharp cutting knife in front of her. "I think they'll be fine," she said as the teakettle began to sing its morning song. "I'll make coffee. Nothing quite like a cup to perk up a cold day and put strength into a body."

It didn't take long for the scent of baking biscuits and fried slices of leftover cornmeal mush topped with fresh eggs to permeate the room. Florence refilled their coffee cups and set the hot biscuits in the center of the table, while Aunt Amelia slid the cornmeal and eggs onto their plates.

While they bowed their heads and gave thanks, an onslaught of rain hit the window with the strength of a full-fledged gale. "It sounds an awful lot like winter," Florence muttered as she picked up a biscuit and buttered it. "Looks like it, too."

The cold rain streamed down the outside of the window, a virtual flood blotting out the countryside. "It'll move on soon." Aunt Amelia took a sip of coffee followed by a forkful of cornmeal and egg. "And in the meantime, the barrels will fill even while we enjoy our breakfast."

Florence nodded, but deep inside she didn't feel thankful. If the rains continued, the road through the canyon would be impassable, especially if the creek rose and flooded the flats.

Restlessness always filled her when the winds blew and rain came down sideways creating rivulets of water on the windowpane. It was her dancing song. She could hear it in the wind's music and in the soughing of the ancient trees. It trembled from the heights—the haunting melody spoke to her senses.

But now, she shivered in spite of the music. Waiting was hard and waiting stifled her song.

"Dreaming again?" her aunt asked.

Florence looked up and smiled. "Kind of," she said as she bit into her biscuit. "Mmm, it's good. I guess my wild whacks didn't matter after all."

"Only if you had kept it up, at least it's what my mother used to say. I never actually experienced it, but Mother loved to tell the story how when she was young and kneaded biscuit dough as though it were yeast bread, her favorite uncle broke a tooth when he bit into it. Who knows? She could've left it too long in the oven."

She stopped abruptly. In the silence came a sound that could be none other than Vaughn chewing on his bone. Aunt Amelia flashed Florence a look to bode no good for any dog, then bent down and looked under the table. But instead of a big, black Vaughn sneaking out with his tail between his legs, Florence heard the thump of his tail.

Aunt Amelia's gaze met Florence's. "I never saw such a look of absolute contentment on the face of either man or beast. No way am I going to break it up."

After breakfast, the two women cleaned up the kitchen in a companionable silence, each busy with her own thoughts and dreams. Later, Florence built a fire in the fireplace, and they got out their sewing projects.

Seated on the sofa in front of the whispering fire, Florence worked on yet another diaper for the expected little one as Aunt Amelia, determined to make Florence's dream of yellow kitchen curtains a reality, basted a ruffle around the bottom and inside edges of the first one. When she finished, she held it up for Florence to see.

Florence smiled and nodded her appreciation. "It's going to be beautiful, Aunt Amelia. A dream fulfilled is what it is to me. I can hardly wait until they're ready to be hung. And Will will be glad, too. He measured the windows and brought home the rods before he left. They're stored in the lean-to up against the shed wall. When the rain lets up, I'll go out and bring the one for the kitchen inside. It will be fun to have them up for winter."

She held high the diaper she had just finished. "This is my twelfth one." She eyed the billowing yellow material destined for curtains. "Do you think I might be able to help on one of the curtains?"

"Why, yes, it would be wonderful," Aunt Amelia exclaimed. "It would speed things up if you baste along the edge of the other ruffle." She reached inside her sewing basket and drew out a folded piece of yellow fabric. "It's all ready to go. It would be nice to have your help."

Florence took the fabric eagerly. She selected a larger needle, threaded it and began weaving it in and out of the fabric as she imagined the new look it would give the kitchen. *Will,* she thought, *when you come home, you're going to love how the yellow brightens the kitchen.*

A stab of pain ripped through her heart. She pursed her lips and decided she'd think about Faye instead. It had been hard to see her return to the other side of the settlement to the shack where she'd been born. Young life was precious, but Faye was older now. Florence's child moved beneath her ribs and she smiled. "You'll have your own place here with us, little one," she murmured.

Aunt Amelia looked up from her sewing. "What did you say? I didn't hear you."

"I was just talking to myself, missing Faye, wondering how she was getting along in school." A sudden rush of love for her aunt surged through her. "I'm so glad you're here with me. If you weren't, I'd be all alone."

"Nonsense. You'd probably up and move into the little house where Dr. Rutler thought I should live." She got to her feet and went over to the window. "I like my space here even if it is a part of your front room. Why, when it's night, all I have to do is pull the blanket we rigged in front of the cot from the tent and I have all the privacy I need."

"You mean you don't miss the tent? I mean, having to put up with me all day and all night." Florence didn't wait for her answer, but stood and turned to face the window. "The rain has stopped," she announced. "The clouds are breaking up."

Aunt Amelia joined her at the window. "We might even have a few sun breaks in the afternoon. I hope so."

"I need a break now," Florence said. She grabbed up a jacket and headed for the door, Vaughn beside her. The wind touched her cheeks. The fresh air exhilarated her.

"Oh, Vaughn, I hear the music—we're going to dance—you and me out behind the barn!"

The evening twilight came, lowering a dusky blanket of peace over the lofty firs and the little cabin snuggled beneath their sheltering branches. Florence, standing at the window, turned as Aunt Amelia came into the front room.

"I think I'll go out for a little while, if you don't need my help right now," she said. "It's been a long time since I waited outside for the coming of the first star."

"You go on ahead, take Vaughn with you," her aunt encouraged. "I've done everything needs doin' in the kitchen." She settled herself into the sofa drawn close to the fireplace and opened the basket with her sewing. "I'd almost like a fire in the fireplace, but no, there's plenty of warmth comin' in from the kitchen stove. I'll be goin' to bed in a bit, anyway."

"Me, too," Florence replied. But when she went looking for Vaughn, she found him stretched out sound asleep beneath the table. She explained to her aunt she hadn't the heart to wake him, then she grabbed up a shawl from the back of the sofa and headed out the door.

As she walked toward the chicken shed, she noted the sound of birds chirping in the underbrush as they settled down to sleep. Anticipating the first star, she rehearsed the lines she had heard from her brother's wife while she lived with them. "Star light, star bright, first star I see tonight. I wish I may, I wish I might . . ."

The sound of chickens suddenly rousted from their perches startled her. She froze. Was there a predator in the chicken house?

She started to run toward them and stopped abruptly. A huge mountain lion clutching her favorite red rooster between his jaws stood directly in her path. They both stood as though paralyzed, face to face, not more than ten feet from each other. She looked into the lion's amber eyes and heard the sound of

Little Red's wings beating against the thick golden-brown fur on the cat's massive chest.

Stay calm, stand your ground, raise your voice, and speak loudly. It was something her father had told her when she was child. Except she had never seen a mountain lion before; she was seeing one now.

She lifted her chin high, and knew her eyes blazed fury with the anger pulsating through her. "Go home," she commanded. "Don't come back. Ever."

Even as she spoke, the mountain lion turned and faded into the bushes. The only noise she heard was the sound of the surviving hens frantically cackling out their fears to one another. There was no other sound. Or if there was, she didn't hear it.

Though terror still held her in its grasp, she knew she had to do something to calm the frightened hens. She went into the lean-to in the back and dipped out some barley. As she scattered the grain, they calmed down immediately. She watched them for a few minutes, then returned to the cabin.

Aunt Amelia looked up as Florence opened the door. "What was all the ruckus about?" she asked.

"It was the mountain lion," she whispered. A lump formed in her throat. "He killed my Little Red. He . . ." She lowered her head. "I can't talk about it right it now except to say, he just stood right there in front of me with my rooster between his jaws, his wings beating helplessly against the lion's chest . . ." The words stuck in her throat, and she burst into tears.

She sank to her knees in front of the sofa and buried her face in her aunt's ample lap. "Oh, Aunt Amelia, what shall I do? For all I know, the mountain lion could come back. Will the same thing happen again?"

"I don't know. But I do know what I think I'd do. Why, I'd wake up that lazy Vaughn, tie a rope around his collar, and stick him close to the chicken house. You told me once that

Tilly said most wild creatures won't come near if there's a dog on the premises."

Florence looked up. "Sounds like a good idea. I'll do it." She grabbed a flannel rag from her apron pocket and wiped her nose. "But first, I have to do something else."

She excused herself to the bedroom, lit a candle, and retrieved an envelope, paper, pen, and ink from the stand by the bed. Her hands shook as she opened the ink bottle. For a moment, she sat very still, then dipped the pen into the ink.

She addressed the envelope: William Nickerson, General Delivery, Seattle, Washington, then began to write:

Dear Will,

My dearly loved husband, how I miss you. This evening I surprised a mountain lion with our favorite red rooster between his jaws on the path to the chicken house. Oh, Will, it was so awful, and I was so scared. But I remembered what my dad told me when I was a little girl. I stood as still as a stone and stared into his amber eyes. Then I commanded him to leave and not come back, and he left. One minute he was there, the next he was gone.

In a few minutes, I'm going back to the chicken house with Vaughn. Aunt Amelia said I should tie him there for the night, but I'm not going to. Instead, I'm going to make him a nice bed and tell him to stay. I'm going to do it now before it gets too dark. I love you, Will, and I'm praying every day that God will return you to us, safe and sound.

Our little one is doing just fine and moves a lot. I'm able to do almost everything except heavy lifting, and it's just a precaution. I'm going out now while the twilight lasts.

Dreaming of you,
Your wife, Florence

P.S. I'm also sending hugs and kisses, and so does little Elizabeth, or is it Lester Lee?

At the bottom, she drew in large and small *O*s for hugs a large and small *X*s for kisses. She put away her supplies and spread the letter flat to give the ink time to dry. When she returned, she'd put it into its envelope to give to Dr. Rutler to mail.

"I'm going back out with Vaughn," she whispered to no one in particular as she draped her shawl around her shoulders to shut out the evening chill. A shiver of apprehension raced through her as she headed for the kitchen to rouse the sleeping dog. Mostly she wanted to just climb into her warm bed and let Vaughn do his job.

"I'll be right back," she told her aunt. She smiled. "My warm bed waits, and it's calling me."

Her aunt nodded. "As mine is me, but I'll wait until you're back. I have only a small cluster of French knots to make, and then—a new day will dawn. Things will look better in the morning."

12

For almost a week, October flaunted her colors, and then the rain came, and a low whining wind began to tear loose the leaves. The open spaces and underbrush boasted variations on the theme of brown, from tawny to creamy chocolate then on to burnt chocolate, while the cold wind blew, piling the flying leaves up against the edges of the trees and salal bushes staying green through it all.

The mountain lion seemed to have moved on, for Florence saw no more signs of its presence even though she and Vaughn diligently searched the area around the chicken house and the nearby paths. Even the chickens seemed more content as long as they had grain and fresh straw.

"Don't you even miss Little Red?" she asked as she scattered their daily grain and refreshed their water container. But the hens went on with their scratching and pecking and paid her no attention whatever, and she had to quiet her heart.

She found, though, it wasn't easy, even when she found simple appealing things: green mosses, a flock of chickadees searching for bugs and whatever they could find on the exposed branches of the underbrush, a squirrel with an acorn in his mouth scuttling to the other side of the tree.

Through those days of cold and driving rain, Florence felt a black tide creeping in upon her. It rose heavy and dark and sinister. It crept to her knees, to her hips, and into her heart, or so it seemed. The day came when she lay down in her bed with sudden chills racing through her body as she closed her eyes and let the icy water engulf her senses.

She wasn't aware when Aunt Amelia sent word to Dr. Rutler to come. He stood beside her bed and took her hand while her aunt pressed spoonfuls of bitter willow tea between her lips.

She heard his voice through the heaviness holding her to the bed. Heard him say, "I do believe she's having a recurrence of last winter's rheumatic episode. She'll need excellent care, and I know you'll give it."

"Will," she whispered as Dr. Rutler placed his hands on her abdomen. "Our baby . . ."

"Your baby is fine, Florence; its movements strong. You don't need to worry about it. You simply need to lie still and swallow whatever fluids your aunt gives you. They'll keep you hydrated until the fever leaves."

He put his hand against her forehead. "Can you tell me how you feel?"

Her words came slow, with great effort. "Awful. Heavy. I ache everywhere." A faint smile touched her lips. "Even my feet and my head. My fingers, too."

She opened her eyes and saw Dr. Rutler's face, distorted and swimming in a dusky haze above her. She quickly closed them and let the darkness come.

Sleep, if only she could sleep.

Day followed night, night followed day, and Florence's fever started to subside. Aunt Amelia brought extra pillows and propped her up in bed. "Tomorrow we can try to get you up to use the commode, but today, well, we'll just do the best we can."

Florence looked down at her hands. "My knuckles are swollen like they were before," she whispered. "Am I going to be crippled up again? How will I take care of our baby when it comes?"

"By doing your best to get well. You did it before; you can do it again. Even Dr. Rutler says the sooner you start moving, the quicker you'll recover. And it means using your hands."

Her aunt picked up a glass of warm milk she'd left on the stand. "I'll help you get started. Just cup both hands, put your fingers around the glass, and hold on tight. All you have to do is bring it up to your mouth. Just remember to drink slowly. It will do both you and the little one good."

Florence wrapped her cupped hands around the glass and lifted it to her lips. Although her hands trembled, she concentrated instead on the warmth of the milk against her tongue as she sipped, savoring each mouthful before she swallowed. *I'm doing this for you, little one. Oh, God, let our baby be all right. Please, God, please.*

As though reading her thoughts, Aunt Amelia spoke up. "You don't need to worry about your baby, Florence. Somehow God has arranged for an unborn child to take what it needs from the mother."

A flicker of relief swept through Florence's being. "And God is in this, too. He knew our baby was alive before either Will or I did. It's a miracle. It really is."

"Remember the scripture describing how God formed us in the darkness of the womb? In the secret places of the earth?"

For a moment, Florence's lips quivered. "He even said He knows all our days, when we get up, and when we lie down. Like now, God knows I'm here in this bed and I've been here for several days. And it didn't even take Him by surprise. He knew everything about me, even when I was in His secret place of promise."

She turned toward her aunt as she lowered the empty glass. She frowned. "Do—do I hear someone coming?"

Aunt Amelia grabbed up the glass and scurried into the front room to look out the window. "It's Martha Moad! I think we're about to have company!"

Florence heard their chatter the moment the two women stepped inside and closed the door behind them. Vaughn rushed from his favorite place at the foot of the bed and into the front room. The sound of his happy "woof" as he threw back his head in a welcoming howl made Florence smile.

Their words drifted into the bedroom.

"I brought a box of quilt material for Florence, not for now, of course, but later," Mrs. Moad said. "I can't help but feel the sooner she uses her hands and fingers, the quicker she'll get them back to normal. I wanted the material I've been hanging on to for so long to be here for her when the moment was right."

Florence looked down at her hands and, with her palms open in front of her, slowly moved her fingers and thumbs upward then backward, a little at a time. With each movement, she pictured the baby's face in her mind's eye.

"Lord," she whispered, "I so long to be able to move the way I did before. Would You please touch my fingers and heal my hands?"

Quite suddenly, she longed for her Bible. She could read from the sitting-up position she had assumed with Aunt Amelia's help, but would she be able to turn the pages?

A great longing welled up inside her as she remembered how blind Bartimaeus had sat begging near the road of Jericho.

When he heard a multitude passing, he had asked what it meant and was told Jesus was passing by.

Immediately he had cried out, "Jesus, Son of David, have mercy on me." The crowd demanded he stop, but he cried again, "Jesus, Son of David, have mercy on me."

But Jesus heard him and He came to him and asked, "What shall I do unto you?"

"Lord," he said, "if I might receive my sight."

And Jesus said to him, "Go thy way, thy faith hath made thee whole."

And quite suddenly, Aunt Amelia and Mrs. Moad were standing by her bed. "We don't want to tire you, my dear," her aunt said, "but we were talking about gathering together material and helping you piece a quilt."

"You mentioned once you loved the Tree of Life quilt you found on the bed after your wedding," Mrs. Moad explained. "And then I wondered if you might enjoy making one with your own hands. Or perhaps an old-fashioned crazy quilt might be easier. Either way, you could choose your colors and, of course, add your own small touches."

A helpless feeling welled up inside Florence. "I—I don't know what to say—except I'm not there yet." Her thoughts raced. *I wish you'd just go away. Forgive me, Lord, I didn't really mean it. Or did I?*

"But you will be," Aunt Amelia exclaimed. "I know you. You won't stay down; you'll be up and around before you know it."

"Your aunt said you enjoyed embroidery. Using a needle would help you regain agility in your fingers and also help pass the time. Besides, I have a pattern for the Tree of Life, the one a lady from our quilting group cut out of a magazine. I'd be glad for you to use it to guide you through the process."

"I—I appreciate your offer. But right now, well, I confess I feel sort of overwhelmed. Is it all right if I just think about it for a little while?"

The two older women looked at each other and both nodded their heads. "Right now, you just need to rest, dear." Aunt Amelia bent over her niece and gently eased the extra pillows out from behind her back. "Just lie flat and take it easy. I'll bring you something more to drink in an hour or so. What you need is nourishment and lots of fluids. We'll talk about quilting later."

The two women quietly slipped from the room. Florence heard the sound of the stove poker lifting the lid and pictured the cups with the tiny pink rosebuds they'd use for tea.

Pink roses, her wedding flowers. But now Will was gone. "Lord Jesus, Son of God, the Great Healer, have mercy on me," she whispered

His answer came from deep within her soul. *What shall I do for you?*

"Lord, if I might be healed, and please, bring Will home to us."

She took several deep breaths and closed her eyes. Then words came again from somewhere deep within her. *Go to sleep, My daughter, wait with Me, your faith has made you whole.*

As she rested in His embrace, peace settled over her restless soul. Her God had spoken; now she could rest.

Florence awakened to the sound of muted voices and the clank of a stove lid in the kitchen. She opened her eyes and noted the light coming through the bedroom window suggested late afternoon or early evening. Her stomach growled and she smiled.

"It's about time you woke up," she murmured to herself even as a young woman with tawny hair tucked in a bun on the top of her head appeared in the doorway. "Tilly!" she cried. "I—It's good to see you. How long have you been here?"

"Not long. I brought your dinner, and just in time, too." She came over to the bed. "Aunt Amelia was fussing over the evening meal when I got here. She'd already laid out the potatoes and was getting ready to cut up a big squash. She looked tired, too."

She bent down, reached for Florence's hand, then held it in both of hers while tears gathered in her eyes. "I'm praying for you, dear one," she said as she gently lifted the hand she held to her lips and kissed each knuckle.

Florence felt her nose tickle and tried to snuff it away. "I always know when I feel like crying, somehow it affects my nose."

Quickly, Tilly pulled a handkerchief from her pocket, formed a loose wad, and held it beneath Florence's nose. She blew hard and they both giggled.

"Still my girl, aren't you?" Florence said.

"I know—I know. Remember how you always had to remind me before I left for school with Faye? Actually, it was you or Aunt Amelia who'd ask the all-important question, 'Do you have a hankie with you?' Then one of you would hand me two, one for Faye and one for me."

"But tell me, Tilly, how did you happen to come tonight? I mean what about Faye? Don't you take her to school each morning?"

"Yes, of course. But Clarence is going to take her for a few days. Actually, when he heard how ill you were, he insisted you and Aunt Amelia needed me here. Practically packed my bag and dragged me out to the wagon."

Tilly leaned forward and touched her lips to Florence's forehead. "You're still running a fever, and I'm glad I could come. Besides," she added, "Dr. Rutler asked me to. He's as worried about Aunt Amelia as much as he is about you. Said she'd be needing help caring for you, at least as long as you were running a fever, and I was the one he wanted to do it."

"He knows it's your gifting, Tilly, a part of who you are. Remember the doctor who applauded the care you gave Irene's sister and her baby who live downriver from here?"

Tilly nodded. "Actually it was sort of a turning point in my life. Before then, I never really thought deeply about my future. I mean, I had the responsibility for Faye, and it consumed me. And then later to find I had a gift for drawing and painting, I don't quite know how it fits into my life, except it's something I must do whether I'm home or caring for someone when they need me; it's a part of who I am."

Aunt Amelia bustled into the room. "You girls goin' to talk your lives away? Why, I'm starved and everything's ready."

Tilly smiled and nodded. "I'll be right there to help. What do you think about bringing our supper in here so the three of us can eat together?"

Vaughn lifted his head and beat his tail against the floor. Aunt Amelia smiled. "I think it's a wonderful idea." She looked at big, black Vaughn and shook her head. "The dog thinks so, too."

What Florence had looked forward to as a solitary meal turned into a party. Her silver wedding tray trimmed with intricate swirls and tiny flowers was the only real tray; the rest were blackened cookie sheets. With a little help from Tilly, she was able to spear the carrots and potatoes and lift them to her mouth. Aunt Amelia gave her a spoon to scoop up the tender roast beef, and Tilly helped her load it.

"This pot roast melts in your mouth," Florence exclaimed.

Afterward, Aunt Amelia insisted on cleaning up alone while "the girls," as she put it, had a chance to chat. "Besides," she added, "I kind of like the good feeling cleanin' up gives me, especially when I don't do the cookin'."

"I found a verse God gave me to give to you," Tilly said when Aunt Amelia left them alone together. "I read it yesterday, and it was as though God underlined it in light. I want to show it to you. It'll encourage you."

Florence gestured toward the stand beside the bed. "Aunt Amelia probably put it in the drawer to make room for other things when I was so sick."

"Ah, here it is," Tilly said as she pulled out the Bible. She sat down on the edge of the bed and leafed through the pages. "It's in Job, chapter fourteen. Here it is. Listen:

"For there is hope of a tree, if it be cut down, that it will sprout again, and that the tender branch thereof will not cease. Though the root thereof wax old in the earth, and the stock thereof die in the ground; Yet through the scent of water it will bud, and bring forth boughs like a plant."

Tilly lifted her head and looked at Florence, her gaze searching. "Does it say something to you, Florence? Perhaps something about you and Will? It's like maybe you see a truth that speaks truth to your heart. I want to know what it is."

Florence nodded and tried unsuccessfully to find the handkerchief in the bed, and wiped her nose against her sleeve. "Why don't you get me a handkerchief, Tilly, even a rag from the rag bag would do. Make it flannel if you can find one. I know I put some in."

Tilly scurried off leaving the Bible behind. Florence's trembling hands tried unsuccessfully to move the Bible so she could read the words for herself.

But Tilly knew what to do. The moment she was back, she pressed a soft flannel rag into Florence's hand and turned the Bible so Florence could read the words for herself.

She read it aloud, slowly, prayerfully, letting its message flood deep into her soul. She took her time while Tilly waited expectantly.

When she finished, she lifted her head. "I think God is reminding me there is hope for me and my family in the same way God brings forth life out of something no one ever expects to live again."

She frowned as she sorted through her thoughts. "And the scent of water. Buds break out when healing rain falls. And Jesus said He was the Water of Life, and He always gives us what we need. Like earlier when He whispered His answer to the prayer I prayed when I asked Him to heal me and bring Will back to us again."

Tilly gasped. "What did He say? Did you really hear His voice?"

Florence smiled. "No, but I heard truth deep in my heart. He said, 'Go to sleep, My daughter, wait with Me, your faith has made you whole.'"

Tilly stood and embraced her friend. "Now I know why God gave me those verses for you. You mustn't forget them, Florence, not ever. And I won't forget them either. The both of us, we'll hold them close inside our hearts forever."

All Florence could do was pat her friend's arms in agreement. She knew Tilly would understand.

13

At night, Florence dreamed. At least, she thought it was a dream.

Before her stretched a huge map of Will's farm. She could see the sharp point of the wooded area thrust out like a piece of pie attached to the larger portion of their land. It lengthened the area facing Grahams Ferry Road and, as Will had put it, "gives a lot of extra road frontage and might be good for something someday, perhaps for our children or even our grandchildren. In the meantime, I'd like to clear it for a sheep pasture."

Someone had sketched in the cabin and the tent plus the spring to the far south. The creek wound around and around as it found its way through the canyon. The map even included the spot where Tilly and Faye had carried their laundry the entire first summer they were in the tent.

She saw the garden filled with squash and pumpkins and bean vines waving from poles cut from the slender branches of the hazelnut bushes. She smiled as she recognized the tree bear who bounced on his bottom when the wind blew. The tall giraffe did his best to compete with the bear in making memories for her and Tilly and Faye and even for Aunt Amelia, who had a hard time seeing animals that exist only in the world of imagination.

The map shifted, changed, and in the center stood a tall tree growing from a stump. It reached forth its branches and she glimpsed birds hiding in the leaves, even the face of a mountain lion peeking out from its place on a limb. A silvery dipper and yes, a heart-shaped garland of pink roses hung on a branch. And Vaughn was there, too, his great head thrown back, his front paws braced against the tree trunk as though he were trying to reach the wild squirrels above.

A bluebird flew over her head, and she looked up. A necklace of pearls, her mother's pearls of promise, encircled the treetop pointing upward to God. The Pearl of Great Price symbolized Jesus above all and over all, king of their hearts and king of their home.

At the bottom of the tree was the verse Tilly had read from Job 14:7 written in her own handwriting and stitched with her own needle with silken green thread. It shone like a promise against the dark brown border and whispered truth to her heart: *There is hope of a tree, if it be cut down, that it will sprout again, and that the tender branch thereof will not cease.*

Then suddenly the birds in the tree flew upward, circling, forever higher and higher, disappearing into the blue sky where she could no longer see them. A cold wind descended. It set the dipper to swinging, tossed the pink roses and pearl necklace downward, and tore the bird nests from the branches. A shower of leaves followed, and the sun stopped shining.

She woke suddenly to the sound of high winds soughing through the majestic firs sheltering the cabin. Its music trembled through the darkness and splattered cold rain against her window. In a spurt of independence, she dug her elbows into the mattress and raised herself up in her bed, then shivered as a gust of wind hit the far end of the cabin. It sounded as though some loose object was being pushed across the boards. She took a deep trembling breath and lay back on her pillows.

As she closed her eyes, her dream of the map sank into darkness. But its memory remained burned into her mind. *If I make my own Tree of Life quilt, and make it come alive, it could become a heritage for our family and future generations like the signature quilt Mrs. Moad showed me on my wedding day.*

A quilt—their hopes and dreams . . . When Will came home, she could present it to him, a labor of love and a lasting token of her commitment. Perhaps it would even give him a glimpse of the trust God had placed in her heart as she waited for his return in a lonely and harsh environment.

Lord, may it be so. I ask it in Your name and for Your glory both now and forevermore. Amen.

<hr>

The next morning Florence shared her dream with Tilly and her aunt. Tilly responded with excitement, but Aunt Amelia frowned.

"You can't possibly put all those things into a quilt," she exclaimed. "How could you? It would be a jumbled mess. When you piece a quilt, you use symbolism. It's why you have patterns. You do know that's why, don't you?"

"I—I don't know what to say, Aunt Amelia. Of course, I'd have to follow a pattern if I chose to make a Tree of Life similar to the one the ladies left for Will and me in our room. Except I've never quilted an entire quilt in my life, and maybe I should start with a crazy quilt. I kind of think Mrs. Moad thought I should."

But Aunt Amelia frowned and shook her head. "You'd rather make a Tree of Life quilt though, I can see it in your eyes. Besides, you told me Will loved the one on your bed."

Florence touched tentative fingertips to her mouth and nodded. "But if I did, there's so much more I'd like to make part of it. Perhaps a bird design in each corner. The first spring we were here, a bluebird pair made a nest in the grove near the spring. In a way, it was my introduction to country life. I don't want to ever forget it."

"You don't need to," Tilly said softly. "It seems to me you need to let your memories work their way in naturally. You know what I'd like you to add?"

Florence shook her head. "Tell me."

"Somewhere there ought to be embroidered ivory silk circles strung together to resemble your mother's pearl necklace." Tilly's blue eyes met Florence's brown ones. "Both of us wore it on our wedding day, and we don't want to ever forget."

A silence followed her words, and it was Aunt Amelia who broke it. "I think we should get out your mother's pearls right now even if it isn't Christmas or a wedding. Seems like we need them."

The two younger women nodded and Florence pointed to the closet. "They're in the very back on the highest shelf."

"I'll get them," Tilly exclaimed as she leaped up to tug open the door. Her voice trailed back to the waiting women. "Florence, you have a straw hat in here and it's adorable. I've never seen you wear it. How come?"

"I guess I forgot," Florence confessed.

And suddenly she was remembering when her trunk had been swept off the steamboat. As she looked back, she saw herself wearing the only clothes she had, as she stood in Hal and Irene's rooms at the back of the store. Irene had packed up a bunch of clothes she could no longer wear and had given them to her.

Two stood out in her mind. One was the pink rosebud silk blouse she had worn when Will came home from Skagway, the other a fashionable straw hat Irene called a boater hat. It seemed like only yesterday when Irene twirled it with her fingers, then gave it to her with a flourish.

She smiled. "Bring it over with the box."

When she returned, Tilly popped the straw hat on top of Florence's dark hair and stood back to look at her.

Florence cocked her head to one side. "What do you think?"

"I think your head is too big," Tilly said. "Somehow it doesn't fit the way it should."

Aunt Amelia agreed. "You've got too much hair, Florence. Why, all it would take would be a strong wind and 'poof.' Why, that little hat would take off like a bluebird flyin'."

"I think you should try it on, Tilly," Florence said. "I have a feeling it might be meant for you, not me."

As Tilly leaned forward and lifted it from her head, Florence saw excitement sparkle her blue eyes. "I know Irene wouldn't care. In fact, I think she'd be delighted to see you wear it."

Tilly adjusted the hat just so on her own blond head and lifted her chin. "How do I look?" she asked.

"You look like a princess," Florence exclaimed. "It does something for your skin and hair. I wonder what Clarence will say when he sees you wearing it."

"But, Florence, Irene gave it to you," Tilly protested. "Perhaps you should put it aside for your own little girl."

But the practical Aunt Amelia would have none of it. "It won't work," she exclaimed. "Why, Florence might be the kind of woman who ends up mothering a brood of boys. Seems to me plain foolish to hang on to to somethin' for someone who isn't even born yet. Especially not when there's someone in the family who could use it."

In a sudden burst of love, Tilly threw her arms around the older woman. "Oh, Aunt Amelia, Faye and me, you really do feel we're part of the same family as your niece, don't you? How can we ever thank you?"

"You don't have to," Aunt Amelia said abruptly. "Just thank Florence and let it go. I know my niece. She's the kind of person who enjoys givin' somethin' she isn't usin' to someone who can, especially when the someone is beside her, givin' her the gift of her time, helpin' her get back on her feet. It's just the way she's made."

Aunt Amelia departed for the kitchen, while Tilly sat down on the edge of the bed and took Florence's hand in hers. "I'm sorry, Florence. What with all the confusion about the hat, we plumb forgot about your mother's pearls."

"Later perhaps?" Florence suggested. "Even though it isn't Christmas, I need to be reminded again what my mother wrote about the desire of her heart; a little girl who would grow up to love her Lord. And I was that little girl."

Tilly nodded. "It's your heritage and mine, too, at least it feels like it is. Shall we do it after the sun goes down? We can light the candles and savor the moment together, just you and me and Aunt Amelia."

"I'd like to," Florence whispered.

Tilly gently lifted her hand in hers and began to massage the stiffened fingers, then gently worked her way up to her elbows. "When I'm not here to do this, I'm going to ask Aunt Amelia and Mrs. Moad to take over. Both Dr. Rutler and I feel if we do this morning and night, you'll recover more quickly. You might even be able to make your dream quilt for Will come true."

"And care for my baby?" Florence whispered.

"Yes," Tilly replied. "But Will will be home then."

For a moment, tears misted Florence's eyes. "But will he? Sometimes I wonder. What if he isn't able to keep his promise?"

"Then God Himself will make a way. It's the kind of God we serve, Florence. Don't ever forget. God isn't finished with you or your family."

She hugged her friend tight, then reached for the straw hat. "I'm going to help Aunt Amelia in the kitchen now," she said. "But every time I look at this darling hat, I'm going to thank God for you and the plans He has for our family. He knows what He's doing, and He does all things well in His time."

She placed the straw hat on top of her tawny hair and smiled at her friend. "Every time I wear this hat, I'll think of you. And when I do, I'll pray."

Tilly turned and headed for the door. Florence smiled as she noted the brave lift of her head and the dried rose she'd stuck in the hat's brim waving courage back at her with each step she took. It was almost like watching a ship setting sail into an unknown sea with sails unfurled and flags blowing in the wind.

Lord, give me courage to face my tomorrows.

Light from the departing sun set the remaining leaves on the vine maple outside Florence's window on fire. She valiantly sipped the warm corn chowder from the cup she held between her hands. "I'm tired of this," she whispered. "Why does everything have to be so hard?"

Slowly, carefully she lowered the cup onto the tray in front of her. Perhaps she could handle the biscuit better. At least if she dropped it, it wouldn't spill. And it didn't. She savored each bite of its warm wheat goodness, then licked the melting butter and honey off her fingertips. By the time Tilly came in with a wet cloth to help her clean up, she felt better.

"Aunt Amelia baked sugar cookies," Tilly announced as she removed the kitchen towel she had draped around Florence's neck and replaced it with a fresh white one. "She's even making some of her famous brown sugar frosting to top them off and make them extra special."

Florence smiled. "Just leave it to my aunt to make a perfect party with hardly any notice. I daresay she'll cover the tray she carries them in on with a piece of red velvet, too. It will be lovely."

"It's a beautiful tradition. I'm just hoping Clarence and I can make some of our own. You know, the kind that lingers in your memory. I know I'll never forget our first Christmas in the tent."

Florence nodded. "Nor I. And next Christmas is only a couple of months away. Will will be home then, and we'll have our newborn little one snuggled in its blanket."

"Your little girl—I just know it's going to be girl," Tilly murmured. A dreamy look shadowed her eyes. "And time goes so fast. Perhaps by next summer Clarence and I will welcome our own baby—a boy or a girl. I wonder if it will happen. If it does, which one will it be? A son or a daughter? Only God knows."

She reached for the matches and lit the candle on Florence's stand. It took only a moment before the wick caught fire. "We need more than one," she said. "I'll get a couple more. Let me take your tray."

As Tilly disappeared through the doorway, Florence felt the baby shift inside her belly. A tiny foot pressed hard against her ribs. As she pressed her palm against the spot, she found herself wondering what their future held. Would Will really be there to welcome their little one at its birth? But why hadn't he written? He'd said he would.

"Oh, God," she whispered as she leaned back on the pillow. "I'm so tired."

As the darkness of evening lowered, she heard a distant coyote let out a long and lonely howl. A second replied, and then the two together chorused in a series of yips. Were the coyotes preparing for a hunt? Would others join them in their chorus?

A deep sense of loneliness swept through her. She was alone, but she wasn't forsaken. She shrugged her shoulders against the pillows as she tried to make herself more comfortable when the baby moved, creating pressure on her left side.

A soft step and Tilly came in carrying two more candles. "It'll push back the darkness." She set one in the window and placed the other alongside the one beside the bed.

"Are you ready for our party?" she asked. "Aunt Amelia is."

Even as she spoke, Aunt Amelia swept in bearing a tray laden with frosted sugar cookies and cups. There was even a sprig of a fir branch tied with a bright red ribbon. And, yes, there was a swath of red velvet folded over her arm. Somehow, Florence knew it would be there.

She watched her aunt set the tray on the foot of the bed and carefully spread the red velvet over Florence's lap. Tilly brought over the small leather chest, with its gold key dangling on a cord attached to the handle, and set it on top of the quilt that served as a spread. Florence caught her breath. This tiny chest had once belonged to her mother.

A solemn hush fell as Aunt Amelia turned the key and opened the leather chest. She popped open the clasp with her fingernail and took out a faded red box. "It's for you to open," she said.

But Florence shook her head. "Not now. But I will on Christmas Eve. I promise."

Tilly pulled up the false bottom and drew out the water-stained note decorated with tiny rosebuds on which Florence's mother had written, *My Greatest Heart's Desire—April 27, 1875.* She unfolded the note and carefully arranged it on the red velvet so her friend could read it.

Florence leaned forward, and with her voice unsteady and filled with emotion, she slowly and carefully read her mother's words aloud: *"I want a little girl who will love Jesus with all her heart. My prayer is that she will find the One who loves her so much that He gave everything He had so she might belong to Him. May the pearl necklace always remind her that she is His precious pearl who gave His life so she might live. His very own beloved daughter."*

"It's about me," she whispered. "My mother wrote it in the spring of 1875, the day before I was born. And I have found Him." She bowed her head in the silence following her words and covered her face with her hands.

"Tilly, we both wrote down the desires of our hearts the Christmas Eve before Will returned from Skagway. Do you want to read yours now?"

But Tilly shook her head. "Not until after Will's and your baby is born. But I can share what I remember most about the night. It was there in the tent I saw Jesus in your life and in Aunt Amelia's."

For a moment, her hand covered her mouth. "Somehow I recognized Him in Faye's face and even in Callie, our crippled outcast mare whose only desire was to serve us. And then He sent Clarence to show Himself through his acts of kindness in the thoughtfulness and kindness he poured out on all of us."

Tilly leaned forward and removed the pearl necklace. She laid it briefly on the red velvet then placed it around Florence's neck.

"Just for tonight," she whispered, "to help you remember. Your hopes and dreams belong to God."

14

First light. It crept softly in through the window, gradually transforming the room a small detail at a time: a chair drawn close to the bed, the stand nearby where she kept her Bible, even the sampler on the wall. Somehow it quieted her spirit, and it became her favorite time of the day, one she shared with her Lord moment by moment as she lay on her pillow.

It was easier then to give her day to Him and remember again He was the God of love and hope and the source of her courage. It was also a time to repeat the verses He had laid on her heart since Will had left her alone at the farm.

Sometimes she whispered them into the silence: "Hebrews thirteen, five. 'For He hath said, I will never leave thee, nor forsake thee.' Job fourteen, seven through nine. 'There is hope of a tree, if it be cut down, that it will sprout again, and that the tender branch thereof will not cease. Though the root thereof wax old in the earth, and the stock thereof die in the ground; Yet through the scent of water it will bud, and bring forth boughs like a plant.'"

She even said her mother's life verse from Colossians and felt God was pleased: "If ye then be risen with Christ, seek those things which are above, where Christ sitteth on the right hand of God. Set your affection on things above, not on things on the earth."

Shortly after, she heard the clank of iron against iron as her aunt stoked up the fire in the kitchen stove. Soon the good smell of frying salt pork and baking powder biscuits from the oven would drift into her room. On some mornings, it might be hot cakes with butter and syrup, on others it would be oatmeal mush flavored with dried apples and cinnamon. Just thinking about it made her mouth water.

Before then, her aunt would come in with a basin of warm water and a washcloth. She'd plump up the pillows under her head and help her to a sitting position. But each day now, Florence needed less help. Her fingers were less stiff as she practiced her needle skills on the cross-stitches she'd used earlier on the pillowcases she'd started the year before.

"Tilly promised me she'd be here later in the morning, so she can help me try my walking skills," she announced as she took the wet washcloth Aunt Amelia handed her and slowly washed her face. Then Aunt Amelia picked up her hand and, finger by finger, massaged them and then both her wrists.

"I think you'll do fine," Aunt Amelia encouraged. "Remember yesterday? Why, you stood beside the bed and balanced yourself with only the help of your cane. You even took a few steps. It's wonderful to see your coordination returning so soon, even if you do shake a bit."

"I want to be able to sit at the table on Thanksgiving Day," Florence confided. "It's only a little over a week away." Her baby pushed up against her rib cage, and she smiled. "I think our baby is trying to say she wants me to spend more time upright. She's probably tired of lying on her back, or is it her tummy?"

But Aunt Amelia was already headed for the kitchen. *What a beautiful lady,* Florence thought. *The next time she comes in, she'll be carrying a tray heaped with good food and a clean towel over her arm to keep me from messing up my nightgown.*

Except it wasn't her aunt who brought in her breakfast tray, it was Tilly. "I came in while you and Aunt Amelia were talking," she said. "I wanted to surprise you by arriving early." She cocked her head to one side. "You're feeling better, aren't you?"

"Yes. I'm hoping to be strong enough to sit at the table on Thanksgiving. Will you be here?"

Tilly shook her head as she set the tray beside the bed. "We're going to Clarence's mother's house in town. It's not exactly what I wanted, but—well—I can see how much it means to him. And his mother, too, of course. I haven't met her yet, you know. She was spending last summer in Boston with her sister and couldn't be there for our wedding, but now she's back . . ."

"Perhaps Gus . . ." Florence's thoughts raced. Hopefully the old trapper who had scooped her up into his arms the year before and carried her to the table would be there. And Dr. Rutler, of course. He'd be sure to spend the afternoon with Aunt Amelia. "I wonder if they'll ever get married," she mused.

"What are you talking about?" Tilly demanded as she tucked a clean dish towel under Florence's chin. "Who's getting married?"

"No one, I guess. I was just wondering who might be here for Thanksgiving. It'll be quieter without you and Clarence. Sort of lonely."

"It'll be hard for me, too," Tilly confessed.

For a moment, silence filled the room, and in the silence, a gunshot sounded close overhead. Terror sliced through Florence as Tilly raced for the door with Aunt Amelia at her heels.

"Someone almost hit the cabin with gunfire!" Aunt Amelia exclaimed. She ran back into the bedroom and grabbed the pistol from the closet. "I'll scare the life out of 'em!" she exclaimed. "Shootin' on our own property. I'll teach 'em a lesson."

She took off running. Almost without thought, Florence pushed back the blankets and, holding tight to the bed's edge slid onto the floor. She crawled toward the front room, and when she reached her cane resting against the wall, she somehow managed to pull herself up.

As she stood trembling, she heard Vaughn's bark coupled with the sound of the blast from Aunt Amelia's pistol. A shout—a scream. Holding tight to her cane she took a step— and then another. Her thoughts raced, trembling, as though trying to keep pace with her knees.

The door opened, and she heard Tilly's gasp as she rushed to her side and reached for her arm. "Everything's okay, Florence. You need to sit down. I'll help you."

At the same moment, Aunt Amelia and Vaughn exploded into the room. "What were those men thinkin', leavin' two women to fare for themselves alone on an isolated farm out in the middle of nowhere?"

"It's my Will you're talking about, Aunt Amelia," Florence said. "But—as I recall it was your idea."

Her aunt's mouth dropped open as she turned from the open door and saw her niece standing beside the sofa gripping her cane and Tilly's arm. She started to speak, but words didn't come as Tilly pulled the rocker close and helped Florence into it.

"What happened?" Florence gasped.

"Must be those confoun' neighbor boys on the back road. You'd think they'd have more sense."

Vaughn whined softly and laid his great head in her lap. Florence's lips quivered as she leaned forward, cupping his dear face between her hands. "Are you glad to have me here?" she whispered as he worshiped her with his adoring gaze.

Aunt Amelia's response was a huff from deep within her. "Forget the food on your tray, Florence. I'm going to whip up some waffles. We need to celebrate."

Her aunt headed for the kitchen, and Florence's gaze met Tilly's. "Mixing up waffles will help her cope and ease her anxiety," Tilly whispered. "And—we'll get to enjoy them. Poor Aunt Amelia. She was upset, especially when Vaughn tore after those boys and grabbed hold of one of the kid's shirts. Then she shouted and the boy screamed."

Aunt Amelia poked her head into the room with a big yellow bowl in the crook of her arm, a dripping spoon in her other hand. "I want you both to know those young'uns won't be back. In a way, I'm sorry I scared them so bad when I shot over their heads. But they gotta learn, they have to, or they're gonna get into big trouble. Trampin' through someone's property and shootin' over the roof of someone's home is nonsense."

She shook her head disdainfully. "They're old enough to know they're on private property, but I think I showed 'em a thing or two." She waved her spoon in their direction. "I just hope my heart slows down a bit. It feels like it's goin' to jump right out of my chest."

But Tilly was nonplussed. "Just cook up those waffles quick-like, Aunt Amelia. It'll calm you down and us, too. And hurry, please. My stomach is growling a lot worse than Vaughn was when he ripped the boy's shirt half off."

Aunt Amelia disappeared into the kitchen, and Tilly followed her with Florence's tray. She brought in an armload of kindling for lighting a fire in the fireplace.

Florence absorbed the sight of the pale November sun as it slanted through the window, painting a gold rug on the rough wood floor. It transformed the colors in the patchwork curtains her aunt had fashioned from the scraps left behind when she and Tilly and even Mrs. Moad had busied themselves cutting the pieces for her Tree of Life quilt. She leaned back in the rocker as she savored one sight after another: the sofa covered with rustic red roses, the deep green of the fir limb hanging just outside the window, the eager flames licking at the kindling and casting its own red and gold into the room.

She was almost surprised when the sound of the waffle iron being turned by Aunt Amelia's efficient hand intruded, as did the scent of vanilla and cinnamon she knew came from the whoosh of the steam rising from the iron and floating into the front room.

It was her aunt who brought in the trays, one at a time. The three women sat together as they said grace and then fell upon their food. Afterward, Florence lifted her face to her aunt and said she was ready now to start sewing the first pieces of the quilt she would present to Will upon his return. "I might have to learn all over again, but now I'm ready to try—this very morning."

Each stitch a dream, each stitch a prayer. Lord, take care of my Will wherever he may be. Remind him of his wife today, and our little one so soon to be born. Keep him safe, our baby, too.

Each stitch a dream, each stitch a prayer. Give Him journey mercies and provide for all his needs as he continues to seek truth. Send those who can help him in his quest. And then . . .

A knock at the door and Florence poked her needle into the quilt square. Vaughn stretched out at her feet, rumbled a warning growl as Tilly scurried into the front room. "We have company!" she exclaimed. She wiped her hands on her apron and opened the door. "May—may I help you?"

The tall, broad-shouldered man standing on the porch gestured toward the two boys accompanying him. "My name is Arnold Baker, and these are my sons, Gerald and Franklin. I'm your neighbor toward the east and a bit north, and we're here to offer an apology. Are you the owner of this property?"

"No," Tilly replied. "It belongs to my friend and her husband, Mr. Nickerson, who is currently elsewhere. Please come inside. His wife is here, and although she's been ill, she would be glad to speak to you and your sons."

Tilly stepped to one side and gestured to Arnold and his sons to enter. Although Arnold seemed confident, the boys obviously weren't. The shorter of the two kept his head down, while the taller boy's lips quivered as he bravely lifted his head and looked Florence squarely in the eye.

"I'm the one who shot the gun, and I'm sorry my brother and me ran," he said. "Neither of us realized we'd wandered onto your land. I'd aimed at a china pheasant and missed—I think the bullet ricocheted off something and headed right over your cabin roof."

He stopped, took a deep breath, then asked. "Will you accept my apology, Missus, Missus—"

"Missus Nickerson. Why, of course I will." Florence held out her hand and he took it. "Will you accept ours, too? I'm sorry our dog ripped your jacket. He's quite well mannered—at least most of the time."

She leaned forward and tapped Vaughn gently on the nose. "Now you settle down, you hear?" She looked up and smiled. "He does his rumbling thing when he's upset."

"But the dog was only doing his job," Mr. Baker protested. "He was simply doing what dogs need to be doing—taking care of their family and guarding their property—and the boys were trespassing. Besides, guns can be dangerous."

"And so can old ladies when they get mad," Aunt Amelia said as she came in from the kitchen. "I'm sorry. I couldn't help but overhear what you said and your courage to tell it like it was. I shouldn't have got my pistol and shot it off over the boys' heads the way I did, either. The way you've taken responsibility for your actions makes me know I need to take responsibility for mine. You're a fine family, and I'm really sorry for what I said and did."

She turned to the boys. "Would you like some hot cocoa and oatmeal cookies? They're fresh from the oven, and cookies are made to share—you, too, Mr. Baker, you're welcome."

Franklin looked up at his father. "Could I—could I go and watch? I mean . . ."

"Go ahead, Son," Arnold said. "But don't get in the way. You hear?"

"I won't. I promise."

His young voice carried into the front room. "I never made hot cocoa before, but Mama did," he confided. He lowered his voice, "She's dead now, but I don't want Dad to hear. It makes him feel sad to think about Mama."

Mr. Baker caught Florence's eye, and she nodded. "She's very wise," she whispered. "Franklin has taken to her, perhaps because of the loss of his own mother. It might prove to be helpful to your family."

"I guess you're right," he said. "She's kind of like a grandmother, isn't she?"

"She's my mother's sister," Florence confided. "I don't know what I would have done without her after my mother died." She held up her hand. "Listen."

Her aunt's voice permeated the room. "Death is hard. It's why we need to do things to remind us of our missing one sometimes. I think she'd like you to know this."

"Do you like to bake cookies?" Franklin asked. "Can I watch while you make the cocoa?"

"Of course you can. All you do is mix sugar and cocoa and a little water in a sauce pan. I always heat the milk first, but it mustn't boil. It takes lots of stirrin'."

Gerald, eager to make friends with the dog who had chased him, got down on his knees in front of Vaughn and gently rubbed the back of his neck. "He's real gentle, Dad." He turned toward Florence. "Could I come back sometime and take him for a walk, do you think?"

"But of course," she exclaimed. "Any chance your family could come for Thanksgiving? Aunt Amelia is a wonderful cook, and we're short on guests. My husband is in Seattle and"—she gestured toward Tilly who had resumed her sewing—"she and her husband will be in Portland. Except for the good doctor, we'll be alone."

Gerald looked up. "Dad, please. I want to spend time with Vaughn—make him my friend. He's one of the most beautiful dogs I've ever seen."

Mr. Baker laughed. "Well, I must admit I'm not much of a cook. Oh, I do fine with a frying pan, and I know how to boil corn on the cob, but pies and cakes, even cookies, are delicacies in our house. I'll talk it over with the boys, and we'll let you know."

"We'll say yes! We'll say yes!" Gerald exclaimed.

By the sudden thump of Vaughn's tail and a paw placed on the boy's knee, they could see the dog thought it was a good idea, too.

15

The day before Thanksgiving, Florence felt the chill in the air before she opened her eyes; even her nose felt unseasonably cold.

She opened her eyes. The sun hadn't yet arrived in all its glory, but she could see a hard coating of whitish fog frozen against the window pane. She shivered and snuggled deeper into the blankets, heard her aunt's footsteps in the next room followed by the sound of a match being struck against the fireplace rocks. In a little while, warmth would wander through the rooms.

Memories intruded: Will rustling up the fires in those early days at the cabin, and whistling as he came back from filling Callie and the goat's feed trough with hay and scattering grain for the chickens. How she missed him. Today was one of those days when doubts tumbled through her mind and for a while threatened to submerge her. Why hadn't he written? Had he received the letter she had impulsively sent off to General Delivery in Seattle? Perhaps not. He could be anywhere, for Seattle was much like Portland, its waterfront and loading dock bordering the bay like an endless strand of pearls.

But, her thoughts whispered, *He knows where I am. It's not something he would have forgotten. Unless he was terribly ill or even injured, perhaps in a place far from civilization. A remote ranch, even herding horses from one isolated valley to another in search of pasture.*

She squirmed this way and that as she tried to relieve the pain settling in her lower back. At the same time, the baby shoved up hard; already there was a tender spot on the edge of her ribs she could feel whenever she pressed her fingers against it. She hoisted her body upward with her elbows and took a deep breath. Relief, blessed relief, but how long would it last? Her arms trembled, and she lowered herself back on her pillow even as she heard a soft step. She looked up; Aunt Amelia stood by the bed clasping and unclasping her rough, chapped hands.

"It's real cold out and guess what?" she announced. "There's a skiff of snow outside and it's only November. Seems unseasonable, but the valley's this way sometimes. One day good weather and the next day the ground and trees are dusted white. Fickle you might say, but I'm mighty glad those Baker boys chopped all the wood last week and piled it outside the door." She stopped abruptly and frowned. "Are you all right? You look—why, you look downright miserable."

Sudden tears sprang into Florence's eyes and she grimaced. "It's my back and the baby pushing so hard against my rib cage. And my hips and knees ache, too. I—how much longer will I be able to stand it, Aunt Amelia? I mean, I have a month yet, and I'm—I'm just so tired."

"Let me see what I can do, child. I daresay you need a change of position. I'll plump up the pillows and get you onto your side. Maybe bring an extra quilt."

Aunt Amelia's actions were as quick as her words, and Florence gave a sigh of relief. "Somehow drawing up my knees

149

a bit eases the pressure on my back and hips and the extra quilt—it's warm—did you have it next to the stove, Aunt Amelia? I feel like a happy bug wrapped in a rug. I really do."

"You look like one, too. Another hour and we'll have breakfast together in front of the fire. How does that sound?"

"Wonderful!" Aunt Amelia grabbed up Florence's cape and tied a wool scarf beneath her chin. "When I come back from caring for the critters, I'll fix a grand breakfast and then start makin' our Thanksgiving pies. I've already cooked up the pumpkin, and yesterday I did up a fresh batch of apple butter to go with the biscuits. You'll see."

And she was gone. Florence heard the door close behind her and took a deep breath. Winter was already challenging their comfort, but together they'd come through just fine. Besides, she had a quilt to create. A stitch, a prayer, another stitch, another stitch, a hope, and a dream. She snuggled deeper into the warm bed. It didn't matter if the snow melted off the tree boughs and grass before she saw it. Instead, she would allow the warmth of the extra quilt to lull her to sleep.

A stitch and a prayer, one for Will, another for me and our baby, Aunt Amelia, our Thanksgiving guests. Her thoughts scattered. *I thank You, heavenly Father . . .*

<hr/>

Thanksgiving Day dawned with dark clouds without even a skiff of snow to mask its shades of brown and gray. The deciduous trees lifted bare branches skyward, their only adornment patches of mosses—some gray and others, various shades of green. The brown cedar fronds had been tossed to the ground when the winds blew, and one could now see light filtering through their branches, particularly when skies were blue or painted with the colors of sunset.

The cabin emanated an aura of celebration and color. Already the table was set with fresh linens and shining silverware and a centerpiece of golden gourds, red apples, shiny brown acorns, and hazelnuts still in their shells. Tilly had fashioned a wreath from twining grapevines. that she'd found on a wood fence by an abandoned shed not far from their home.

"I trimmed it with white snow berries and red rose hips I gleaned from the woods, but at Christmastime it can be decorated with holly and evergreen boughs," she had said as she pounded in a nail on which to hang her gift. "It will proclaim joy to all your guests. Perhaps Clarence can shoot down a sprig of mistletoe from the ancient oak on the slope on the other side of the canyon. He tells me he's done it before."

Florence sighed. This year there would be no Tilly or Faye to grace their table. No Will either. But there would be others: Dr. Rutler, Arnold Baker and his two sons, and John and Martha Moad.

"There'll be eight of us," Aunt Amelia exclaimed. "The perfect number to fit comfortable around the table. But," she added, "we can stretch it just fine if Trapper Gus shows."

Dr. Rutler was the first to arrive. Florence could hear the sound of his mare's hooves against the hard-packed road as he came up out of the canyon toward the cabin. Eager for him to see the improvement she'd made, she put her sewing aside and reached for her cane. Although her ankles still felt weak, she walked one step at a time with her aunt close behind her. But it was she who opened the door.

"Florence," he exclaimed. "You're better, much better." He turned to Aunt Amelia, and for a minute Florence thought he might hug her. "Excellent nursing! Excellent care," he put both hands on her shoulders and looked down at her. "I knew you and Tilly could pull it off. You're a great team, and I daresay you had help from the patient herself."

"Yes, we did. But most of all we had help from the Great Physician Himself." Aunt Amelia stepped back a step and gasped. "Oh dear," she cried, "my potatoes!" She turned and ran into the kitchen.

A tender smile swept across Dr. Rutler's face as he took Florence's arm. "I have something to give you, something important. Let's get you settled in your chair. You are using the rocker aren't you?"

"Yes, it's comfortable and reassuring somehow. Aunt Amelia and Tilly, when she was here, massaged my fingers every day when they were so stiff. Now I'm learning to make them use a needle, but it's hard work."

She sank into the rocking chair and continued. "I'm practicing my stitches every day, and both Tilly and Aunt Amelia—and yes, even Martha Moad—have been encouraging me." In her earnestness, she leaned forward and clasped her hands together. "I'm making a quilt to give to Will when he comes home. It's a Tree of Life, like the one the church gave us, but it's going to be different. I'm going to make a special centerpiece with a tree growing out of a stump. There'll be birds and nests in the limbs, and there's a verse—"

She stopped abruptly as the doctor removed a letter from his coat pocket and handed it to her. "Hal gave it to me when I stopped at the store yesterday. It's postmarked Seattle and addressed to you. Here, let me open it."

He leaned over, slit it with his pocket knife, then disappeared into the kitchen leaving Florence holding the envelope between fingers that suddenly refused to obey when she tried to remove the folded sheet of paper inside. She took a deep breath, closed her eyes to calm herself, and waited while a prayer formed in her heart. *Please, Lord, help me.*

She took another deep breath and opened her eyes. Her fingers trembled as she unfolded the letter.

My beloved wife,

I'm so sorry I left you to deal with the mountain lion alone. When I read your letter, I got goose bumps. You are one brave woman who kept her head and displayed courage and wisdom.

The strangest thing about my getting your letter was that I had gone to the main post office in Seattle to mail a letter for a friend. I told the postmaster who I was, and he looked at me so funny. "I have a letter for you, sir," he said, and he gave me the letter you wrote. I told him I didn't deserve you. And I don't. Leaving you alone and then the loss of your favorite rooster, Little Red. I'm sorry. But I think what happened at the post office was a miracle, don't you?

Florence, please, please remember my promise. I will be at your side when our baby is born. Nothing will keep me away.

Your loving husband, Will

Florence carefully refolded the letter and slid it into the envelope. As she slipped it into her bodice, she wondered if she'd be able to control her emotions. Tears mixed with hope and fear, tears that threatened to overflow. But she mustn't spoil Thanksgiving for Aunt Amelia or their guests.

Thankfully, she heard the sound of an approaching wagon and lifted her head. The Moads, it had to be. Dr. Rutler came in from the kitchen and gave her a searching look.

"I'm okay," she whispered. "And thank you for the letter."

He nodded and smiled and went out to help their guests disembark. Then Dr. Rutler brought in the great baked turkey, and Martha followed with a basket of goodies. Florence could only guess at what might be inside. Stuffing, perhaps cranberry sauce. Her mouth watered in expectation even though her heart felt ready to break. What was it Aunt Amelia had said? Hearts don't break, they just get bigger and better, if you don't get bitter. Thinking about it made her smile as she remembered how they'd laughed together over the bigger, better, and bitter.

The door opened and John came in. He, too, carried a big basket. "Martha says you can have these pieces of material she's been hanging on to all these years. Says you're making a memory quilt." He set the basket on the floor beside her and lifted the lid.

Florence gasped. "The colors!" she exclaimed. "I see lots of greens and white, too. And browns—there's some of those, too. It's almost as if she's been reading my mind, or else looking over my shoulder."

"Oh, my Martha has boxes and baskets galore of this kind of stuff. Whatever you'll need, I'm sure she'll have it." He shook his head. "And I wouldn't mind a bit getting rid of some more. So, if you need a different assortment of prints, plaids, or other colors, be sure and let us know. We're happy to help."

He went back outside to tend the horses, and Martha returned to the front room. "I asked John to bring the boxes; thought maybe you'd enjoy going through some more of my scraps."

"It's not just scraps you've given me, it's far more," Florence said. "I'm starting, you know. I want you to see the swath of dark green Tilly cut from the large fabric piece you brought over earlier. It took me a couple of days to do it, but I was able to write the scripture I'm using to tie the quilt theme together." She smiled. "I even started to embroider it, although I haven't gotten much past the first word."

"I'd love to see it, my dear. Perhaps after dinner the three of us girls can get together and you can show us. And if there's anything I can do to help . . ."

Vaughn growled and ran to the door just as John came in. "I think I spotted your new friends coming across the field; your dog did, too," he said. "Looks like he's on his way to meet them. Is it all right?"

"It's fine," Florence reassured. "It's only been a week or two since we've met them, and already Vaughn and the boys especially are great friends. They've come several times to help with chores. It has helped Aunt Amelia, what with Tilly and Clarence out of town, and so much ending up on her shoulders. Why, they chopped wood and made kindling and stayed till almost dark so they could clean out the chicken pen."

John nodded slowly, his head moving up and down with his thoughts. "The world needs more young people like them," he said. "Why, I remember—"

The door swung open with a bang, and Franklin raced headlong through the front room and into the kitchen. "Aunt Amelia!" he cried. "The mountain lion—he killed my favorite lamb, the one Gerald and I fed with a bottle! He dragged her into the woods!"

Florence covered her face with her hands and bowed her head while her thoughts raced uncontrollably. A pet lamb and a little red rooster. Why did the horrid cat go for the pets? It didn't make sense. *God, why did You let it happen?*

Deep within her spirit, she heard His answer. *Your thoughts are not My thoughts, Your ways are not My ways. As the heavens are higher than the earth, so are My ways higher than your ways, and My thoughts than your thoughts.*

She lifted her head. The two silent men in the front room with Gerald beside were watching her in alarm.

"It's sad, isn't it?" she said, "but I'm glad Aunt Amelia is there for little Franklin. He needs her." *And I need her, too*, she wanted to say, but didn't.

Instead, she looked from one worried face to another. "Arnold, I'd like to introduce you and your son to our friend John Moad, who lives a mile or so south of us on Grahams Ferry Road." She smiled at John. "And this is Arnold Baker and his son Gerald. The younger boy who ran past us is also his. His name is Franklin."

She took a deep breath. "Did I do it all right, or did I mix it up? It's been a long time since I've been out with people, even longer since I read an etiquette book."

The men laughed and the tension broke. "You did just fine, Florence, just fine," John said, as the three of them exchanged handshakes and big grins.

Just then, Dr. Rutler and Martha came into the room. "I'm Martha Moad, John's wife, and I already know who you are. You're Arnold Baker, and your oldest son is Gerald. I've already met your little Franklin. He's a charmer."

"Even when he's crying?" Arnold asked.

"Oh, yes," Martha continued. "He's absolutely adorable, and he has such a soft heart. He feels things deeply, and Aunt Amelia is so good for him. He needed her motherly touch, and she has it, even though she's never had a child."

"It's because there's so many motherless children in the world," Florence said. "When my parents died, she was there for me. I'll never forget. Never."

Martha smiled and nodded and turned in Dr. Rutler's direction. "This man is the good doctor, and he lives up to his reputation. Dr. Rutler is well-known in the community. Oh, I almost forgot. Aunt Amelia said to tell you, our dinner will be a bit late but not to worry. It will be ready soon."

"Tell her not to worry about us," John said. "I have a couple of boxes out in the wagon that need bringing in, and I'd like to take a look around." He nodded at Gerald. "We could go see the chicken shed you cleaned out the other day, too. Maybe even find something else to be done and lend a hand."

The four men disappeared through the door into the chilly November day. Martha looked after them. "Good men," she said. "Very good men."

She turned to Florence. "Now would be a good time to show me the verse you're embroidering. I'd love to see how it's coming along, but most of all I want to hear the quilt tell its story. Do you know what I mean?"

Florence smiled at her. "Yes, I do. Just bring me the basket beside the bed, and I'll show you my dream. Are you ready to listen?"

And Martha nodded. "I am. Perhaps we'll hear it best as we share it with each other."

16

Tilly had cut the border for the quilt, and Florence's heart leapt in anticipation as Martha smoothed the strip of brown fabric across the back of the sofa. "Why, this is going to be beautiful," she murmured, as her fingertips lightly traced the scripture Florence had so painstakingly written in chalk. She returned to the beginning and smoothed the silk forest-green stitches Florence had used to create the first word.

"My stitches are a bit uneven," Florence whispered, "but I did the best I could. Do you think I should take them out and try again later when my fingers improve?"

Martha shook her head. "No, leave them. They have a message of their own, Florence, and each stitch communicates what's in your heart. Will likely will treasure it forever, as should your children and grandchildren some day."

"Finishing it is going to take a long time, Martha." She sighed. "I had such visions of presenting a completed quilt to Will when he returns. I know now, even if by some miracle I could sew around the clock, I will have only just begun."

"My dear, you definitely have your family and me to help with the piecing. I could even ask the ladies in the church to help; they love doing this sort of thing."

"But even then . . ."

"Yes, I know. It will be next to impossible to piece a complete quilt in such a time span. When I looked back into the generations preceding us, I became aware of what it took to create a quilt that would become an heirloom to future generations. Some of those unfinished quilts were even handed down from mother to daughter and then to granddaughter. Some were never finished."

She folded the border into a neat square. "Did you say something about inserting a centerpiece?"

Florence nodded. "It isn't a part of the pattern you gave me. But it is all right to change it, isn't it? Aunt Amelia thought it would work and so did Tilly."

"I say it's just fine. Every quilt is unique, Florence. If you can work it in, go for it. You're making an heirloom quilt with its own story to tell."

"The design is something Tilly and Aunt Amelia worked out together: me with the idea, Tilly with her drawing board, and Aunt Amelia with her scissors. The cutouts are in the basket folded inside the cream-colored material I plan to use as the centerpiece. In a way, I see it as the heart of the quilt. So many dreams, so many memories . . ."

Martha laid the border on the back of the sofa and took the material out of the basket. As she unfolded it, Florence held her breath, her thoughts racing. *I hope she likes it—hope I can find words to explain so she'll understand.*

Martha held up the dipper, the frog, and a cluster of pale lavender Mayflowers on long slender stems. "It's the spring on the side of the hill isn't it? Are you going to embroider the paw prints of the animals that come to drink?"

Florence nodded. "Our tent and the cabin will be in miniature clouds in the sky above the tree. And Callie. We have to have Callie and the tree—"

"The tree? What tree?"

"The one I wrote about around the border from Job, except I left out some of the words so they'll fit right. Let me see if I can say it by heart the way I wrote it on the border pieces: 'There is hope of a tree, if it be cut down, that it will sprout again, and that its tender branch will not cease . . . at the scent of water it will bud . . . and bring forth boughs.'"

She looked up. "Tilly made the tree in the verse in such a way that it can be attached onto the centerpiece in pieces to create a tree growing out of a stump."

"Oh, now I understand. But—but my goodness, child, how do you plan to attach them?"

"A piece at a time. I want to come to the place where I can do creamy French knots for the pearl necklace I see at the top of the tree, then solid stitching to fill in the petals and leaves of the woodland flowers. Will told me about them when he described the farm he bought the night he asked me to be his wife. But first, I'm just going to attach the cutouts with simple stitches like the one I'm using now to outline the words of the scripture. The rest will come later—I hope."

Martha didn't appear to be listening. She was too busy putting the tree together and arranging the various objects around and it and in it. "This is wonderful!" she exclaimed. "Like a puzzle. So fascinating, so original."

Aunt Amelia, with Franklin at her heels, stepped into the room. "It's time to eat," she announced. "Everything is ready. Except carving the turkey. Will your John do it for us, do you think?"

Martha looked up, startled. "Why—oh my, I forgot to come and help. I'm sorry I—really I am. I guess I got carried away."

She scurried to the door and shouted. "John, John, we need you to carve the big bird! Can you come?"

She heard an answering shout and hurried to the kitchen. "They're coming. Now, what can I do to help in here. Surely there's something . . ."

Franklin slowly sidled up to Florence. He hesitated a moment, then asked. "Can I put your cutouts in the basket for you?"

Florence nodded. "I'd appreciate it if you would. It's difficult for me to get up and down, and I . . ."

"Don't worry," he reassured her. "I'll take good care of them, Mrs. Nickerson. You can trust me."

"I know I can, and I thank you, too. It's wonderful to have you here with us. Are you hungry?"

A secret smile slid across his face. "Yes, and it smells good, too, especially the apple butter. I wanted to take a swipe of it with a spoon, but I didn't."

He carefully stacked the tree pieces, then followed up with the smaller ones. "I like the frog best," he confided as he lifted it to his ear. "I think I hear him croak."

"You just might," she said. "After all, those pieces have a story to tell. You just might be the first one to hear it speak."

The woman and the boy exchanged a wink and a smile. The quilt pieces were neatly stacked in the basket when the men had returned and were awaiting their turn at the wash-stand in the corner of the kitchen. John stood at the stove, placing slices of white and brown meat onto a big white platter. He set the dish on the tablecloth in the middle of the table and gave Franklin and Gerald an approving smile as they escorted Florence to a chair at the end.

Their Thanksgiving meal was ready, and so were the people.

Dr. Rutler's gaze searched the faces of those seated at the table. "Before we thank God for this bountiful spread, I ask you to take the hand of the ones nearest you and tell at least two things you are thankful for this day. Who would like to start?"

Franklin raised his hand and shouted, "I do! I do! Please choose me!"

Dr. Rutler nodded at the small boy. "You're chosen, Franklin."

The boy raised his chin. "Most of all I'm thankful for my Aunt Amelia. She lets me remember my mother. Sometimes it makes me cry, but she said it was all right, it was God blessing me. I think maybe she's right."

Florence felt tears sting her eyes, saw Dr. Rutler nod at her. "That's a hard one to follow," she said in a voice trying hard not to tremble. She picked up her napkin and wiped her nose. "Most of all I'm thankful for my husband, a God who loves me, and for friends who encourage me. And our baby. To think it still lives. A miracle sent to us by God Himself."

Martha spoke next. "I'm thankful for my husband, too, and good neighbors: Aunt Amelia's family and now the Bakers."

John was short and to the point. "God and my wife first and little Faye. She wound me around her finger, and it felt good."

"I'm thankful for Will and Florence's new baby, soon to arrive," Dr. Rutler said. "Glad I get to be a part of it, and of course, there's Aunt Amelia."

Everyone laughed.

Aunt Amelia spoke up loud and clear. "I just love bein' part of a family. And cookin' for folks. I like food, and God's given us plenty of it."

Everybody cheered and clapped, and Franklin clapped loudest of all.

Gerald was next. "I'm thankful for the canyon, the trees, and the animals. And our neighbors, too. I like 'em a lot."

"I guess I might say, forgiveness," Arnold said thoughtfully. "And a God who teaches us how to accept it for ourselves and then give it away to others."

The room stilled and Dr. Rutler spoke into the silence. "Our heavenly Father, we come into Your presence to thank You for the many blessings You have bestowed upon us, Your people. We thank You for our freedom here in America and for friends and neighbors. For gardens to give us food for our tables. We rest in You, knowing You are all wise and good, and we can trust You in the light and in the night. You are the One who covers us with Your hand and leads us to still waters and now to this bountiful table. Bless this food to our bodies and us to Your service. Amen."

The tender slices of roast turkey and cranberry sauce, the green beans and mashed potatoes loaded with butter, and Martha's pickled beets began to circle the table. Right away, Florence noticed Franklin carefully buttering a lone biscuit sitting on his plate. He put down his knife, picked up a spoon loaded with apple butter, and carefully spread it over the biscuit he had so carefully buttered. He caught her eye and grinned as he took a huge bite.

She, too, reached for a hot biscuit from the basket when it came to her. She split it open, spread it with butter, then followed with a heaping spoonful of the apple butter spiced with cinnamon and ground cloves. The conversation was a bit like apple butter, too, Florence decided. The perfect spice made everything taste wonderful, at least she thought it did.

After the meal, Aunt Amelia and Martha gathered up the dishes and took care of the leftovers while the men headed out to the porch. At the door, Dr. Rutler turned to Florence. "Would you like to join us? The fresh air would do you good, you know. It would be my privilege to escort you."

"Are you sure, Dr. Rutler? I don't want to be a bother." But even as Florence said the words, a longing rose up inside her. "But I'd love to get out, even if for a little while."

Gerald dashed back into the cabin. "I'll bring a chair," he volunteered.

The good doctor snatched up a shawl from the back of the couch and handed Florence her cane. He guided her to the chair Gerald put by the door, and she sank into it breathing the cool air deep into her lungs. The canyon spread before her without a windowsill to limit the view. The tall firs high above moved restlessly, shifting their branches in a breeze far above her head. Peace settled over her spirit.

But soon the men seemed to forget she was there, and she wished she was with the women instead. All the men could talk about was the mountain lion.

"I think we ought to hike over to your farm, Arnold, and see if we can spot the critter," John said. "I don't much like the idea of it being so close to civilization."

"It's a drain on a lot of us farmers," Arnold agreed. "There's been a lot of talk about a mountain lion coming down from the hills behind us with a taste for chicken and sheep, even taking down a half-grown calf. If we don't do something, we might lose more stock."

"Maybe we could shoot a few rounds into the woods, Dad," Gerald said. "It might scare it and keep it from coming back for more sheep."

"Perhaps so," Arnold replied. "But I don't know. For one thing, a yearling's pretty big. Seems like I remember hearing they hide their kill somewhere at a safe distance and don't go out again until they're hungry. It could take several days."

"But we have coyotes around here," John said. "Lots of them. I've known them to band together and claim a large carcass as their own."

"Seems like sheep are a favorite for the big cats," Arnold observed. "Like I said, once they get a taste of them, they keep coming back. I don't know for sure if it's true or not though."

"I don't like having them nearby," Dr. Rutler said. "They're a threat to our women and children. Look at how the lion scared Florence when she was feeding her chickens a while back. In my opinion, it needs to be put down—for good."

Dr. Rutler turned to Florence as though he suddenly remembered her presence. "I think I'd enjoy a tramp in the woods, maybe work off some of all the good food." He patted his stomach. "What a meal! Our ladies outdid themselves, for sure. Ready to go inside?"

She smiled up at him. "No, but I will. It's a bit chilly out here."

"Perhaps it is best if you went in now," he said. He gave her his arm and helped her stand. "We don't want to overdo a good thing, now, do we?"

"No, but it made a nice interlude, and I thank you." She turned to the men. "Thank you for letting me intrude on your party. If you go after the lion, I'll be praying. So be careful, please. You're each one important to me."

At the door she turned. "Be sure Vaughn goes with you. You might need him."

Franklin reached out his arm and drew Vaughn's head close to his chest. "Do they eat dogs, too? I'd feel terrible if he hurt Florence's dog."

His father reassured him. "I doubt he'd dare do that. Cats don't like dogs much. It seems to me, we don't have to worry. Vaughn knows how to fare for himself. If he doesn't, we'll be nearby."

Dr. Rutler settled Florence into her chair and went into the kitchen with John to tell the women what they'd decided to do.

"It sounds like the best thing to do under the circumstances," Martha said, and Aunt Amelia agreed.

"We're families around here, and the mountain lion needs to leave, one way or the other. We have a gun if you need another weapon."

―∞∞∞―

A dull fear settled over Florence as she picked up her needle and began to outline the next word of the tree verse. Each stitch a prayer: *Lord, I know Will needs You wherever he is. Hold him up and give him something special for which to give You thanks today.*

Another stitch, another prayer: *We need You to protect us and our critters. Be especially near to our men who are getting ready to track down the mountain lion who took the life of Little Red and now Gerald and Franklin's yearling lamb.*

Another stitch, another prayer: *Our men, Dr. Rutler, John, and Arnold.* Another stitch, another prayer: *Gerald and Franklin who went with them. So young they are, so fragile somehow. Bring good into their lives through this new loss.*

She laid her sewing on the table. "I'm getting nervous," she said as her aunt and Martha joined her in front of the fireplace.

"Worried about the menfolk, are you?" Martha asked. "They'll take care of themselves and one another, Vaughn, too. You know they will." She reached into the basket, took out an unfinished square, and began to stitch.

Florence watched her friend's flying fingers and the flash of her needle as it pulled the thread in and out through the fabric. A rush of envy lurched through her being. *It's not fair,* her thoughts whispered. *When she sews, it looks so easy. And her stitches are beautiful.*

And then another voice, this one her Aunt Amelia's: "You'll soon be stitchin' faster than the two of us together. You just have to wait."

Florence sighed. "I know. In the meantime, would you be comfortable if I went out on the porch for a bit more fresh air and maybe some fresh courage? Dr. Rutler was with me earlier, but I think I'd do just fine by myself as long as I take my cane."

The older women looked at each other and nodded. Martha set her sewing down and pushed the nearest chair out onto the porch. Florence thanked her and slowly stood. Aunt Amelia made sure her shawl was tucked around her just so, as Florence reached for her cane. "Every time I do this, it makes my ankles seem a bit stronger."

The door closed behind her, and the great outdoors welcomed her. *It's like coming home,* she thought as the presence of those she loved reached out to her. *And Will may soon be coming home, too. I just have to wait.*

Last night she'd wakened in the night with a verse about waiting that she really didn't want to think about. She even remembered the reference, Isaiah 40:31: *But they that wait upon the LORD shall renew their strength; they shall mount up with wings as eagles; they shall run, and not be weary; and they shall walk, and not faint.*

"But I don't like to wait," she whispered. "Nobody does, do they?"

Instead of sinking into the chair, she walked to the edge of the porch and put her hands on the rail Will had built. In the following silence, she heard the sound of wings and looked up to see a huge eagle dipping low above her head. She felt the soft stir of wind beneath its wings, heard the flutter of its feathers as it circled over her, flying into the tall firs at the top of the canyon. A sense of awe flooded her being. Only God could have guided the eagle so close at this moment. Only God . . .

She stood still and waited. But the eagle didn't return. Instead, she heard the sound of Vaughn baying as though he'd caught the scent of a wild creature. The sound floated across the woods, the swale, and through the garden. She shivered as she pictured her beautiful pet with his head thrown back, his front paws clawing at the foot of a tree. Had he caught the scent of a raccoon, or had he treed the mountain lion? A sudden chill made the back of her arms tingle with apprehension. She shivered.

Vaughn suddenly stopped his baying, and she heard a gunshot. Silence—another shot rang out. This time the door sprang open, and Aunt Amelia was beside her, with Martha close behind.

"I heard a gunshot. You need to come in. Now." Aunt Amelia grabbed Florence's arm. "Why, child, you're as cold as ice. Are you all right?"

"I heard Vaughn baying like a hound who'd treed a wild creature. I—of course I thought of the mountain lion. Oh, Aunt Amelia, you don't suppose?"

"I don't know. But we need to go inside. It's the best place to be when there's shootin' nearby."

The older women took up their sewing, but Florence lingered at the window. She watched the November twilight descend and the clouds reflect the last rays of the sun, transforming them into a pale pink reminding her of half-forgotten strawberry frosting made with egg whites whipped high into delicious peaks of delight.

As the pink faded and shadows lengthened, Florence heard men's laughter and the sound of boys' feet as Gerald and Franklin raced ahead of them across the porch. Franklin headed for Aunt Amelia, and Gerald was right behind.

"I don't think going after him was such a good idea after all," Gerald said. "He was beautiful up there stretched out on the limb. And now," he pressed his lips together and shook his head.

Franklin finished his sentence. "Now he's just dead." And he dove into Aunt Amelia's outstretched arms.

"There's nothing else you could do, Franklin," she said as she gently smoothed the errant curls stuck up every which way on the top of his head. "Nor can you, Gerald. We have to understand that God ordained our men to be protectors of their homes. The mountain lion was a threat to the safety of their wives and children, indeed the greater community. Without animals to sell and butcher for food, families would eventually go without. I don't think there's a man alive who wouldn't have done what our men did today."

"I respect each one of those guys," Gerald said. "I really do. I wonder if I'll grow up to be a strong man like them. I don't especially want to."

"I don't think I wanna grow up," Franklin blurted. "I think I wanna go home."

Arnold must have heard his son's words, for he was the first one in. He took his son in his arms and reached inside the pocket of his overalls for a red kerchief to wipe away Franklin's tears. "We'll talk about it when we get home."

"You best hurry and beat the darkness," Aunt Amelia encouraged.

"Did you bring a lantern to see your way home?" Florence asked. "If you didn't, you can use ours. We have two."

Slowly the group scattered. The Bakers crossed the field on foot with Aunt Amelia's lantern to light the way, John and Martha in an almost-empty wagon descending into the canyon. They heard the sound of horses' hooves echoing in the silence as John hurried them up the hill on the other side.

When the cabin was quiet, Dr. Rutler examined Florence. "The baby is a healthy one," he said as he placed his stethoscope on the abdomen. "Does it always move around like this?"

"Off and on, mostly at night, I think," Florence said.

"It may quiet down a bit the last couple of weeks or so before it's born. Are you all ready?"

"Not until Will comes home," she said. "He promised to be here, and he always keeps his promises."

"I agree that Will is trustworthy. But sometimes things happen. However, knowing Will like I do, I'd say he'd brave hell or high water to be at your side. Just keep waiting and praying. I know you will."

For a moment, tears stung Florence's eyes. "Yes," she whispered. She pressed her lips together as she struggled to control their trembling. "And as I do, I'll wait, and pray." *Each stitch a prayer, each prayer a hope. Lord, take care of my man.*

17

Cold winter rain and winds set in the moment the calendar changed from November to December. Sometimes it even blew smoke down into the front room through the fireplace. "Too bad we can't attach a door to keep it from fillin' our lungs with smoke," Aunt Amelia complained as she hurried to open the front door for the second time in one day. "It's goin' to be the death of us by next spring if it keeps up. And the new baby, comin' soon. New lungs and all, it won't do it any good, for sure."

"I already mentioned it to Dr. Rutler," Florence said. "He thinks he knows where there's a tin piece to fit over the top of the stovepipe, which will do the trick. He says he'll order it from Hal. Maybe he even has one on hand he can send over."

But Aunt Amelia was in a complaining mood and could not be silenced. "Maybe so, but I'm not countin' on it. Men—you can't always trust they'll do what they say they'll do. He'll probably forget or somethin'. Men do that a lot."

"And so do women," Florence said tartly and wondered why she felt like throwing something at her beloved aunt.

It turned out Florence was right. In the afternoon, Dr. Rutler showed up to work on their roof, and Aunt Amelia stood corrected. "He looks like a stooped-shouldered Santa Claus up there," she grumbled. "But I shouldn't have said what I did. Dr. Rutler is a good man. He's done a lot for both of us."

But Florence's ire was up. "He has a crush on you, Aunt Amelia, and you need to treat him better. Not only is he good-looking, but he cares about his patients. Maybe you just need to get sick. You'd change your mind about him in a hurry, then. At least, I hope so."

Aunt Amelia stared at her without a word and then slipped out the door. Florence resumed her sewing, but she stopped and listened when she heard her aunt call up to him. "Come in as soon as you're finished. I've got coffee, and it's fresh. Biscuits, too. I'll just pop them in the oven, and they'll make a mighty good snack, what with my famous apple butter."

Vaughn lifted his head and let out a "ruff" from underneath her chair. "You agree, don't you, Vaughn?" He gave another "ruff" and Florence laughed.

Another burst of wind hit the cabin, and the door swung open to admit Tilly. She took a deep breath, pulled off her wet scarf, removed a packet from beneath her coat, and laid them across the back of the sofa in front of the fireplace. Her coat followed and then her shoes and socks.

"You can't believe how wet it is out there," she exclaimed. "And I have to go back to pick up Faye from school. I hope Sugar will be able to handle all this wind and rain."

"Who's Sugar?"

"The new horse Clarence bought. I know it's a funny name for a horse, but it fits. She's a real sweetie."

Florence smiled. But her smile turned into a frown. "Did you see Dr. Rutler up on the roof when you came in?"

"No. He was coming down the ladder, and guess who was standing there steadying it so he wouldn't end up in a heap on the ground? Why, Aunt Amelia, of course!"

"She's repenting, I think." A laugh bubbled up inside her. "And why did you come clear out here when you have to go back so soon? It's mid-morning already."

"I know. But I'm here on a mission of love, and it's exciting. I had to come." She sat back and folded her hands in her lap. "Yesterday when I brought your centerpiece to show the quilting bee at the Frog Pond Church. They got all excited. In the four hours we were there, those ladies took turns as they embroidered the paw prints and attached the dipper and the birds."

She reached behind her for the packet. "I brought it so you can see it for yourself." She drew out the centerpiece, unfolding it even as she spoke. "I explained that you wanted to have it finished as a gift to your dear Will, but you were beginning to fear you wouldn't be able to finish in time. Then those dear ladies came up with an idea for a circle of love. They want to keep the centerpiece at the church for two weeks, with each woman who wants to help coming in for two hours a day for two weeks. Everyone who wanted to participate was invited to sign up for two hours during the day to come to the church and sew. Then the stitches wouldn't cease and neither would their prayers, except for evenings and early mornings."

"But, but, it's already a prayer quilt," Florence protested. She fought back sudden tears. "I mean—each stitch a prayer, a hope, a dream. Do they understand that?"

"Yes, Florence, they do. They've already committed to pray for Will and for you and the baby, too. The ones who couldn't do it didn't sign, but those who did"—Tilly leaned toward her in her earnestness—"those ladies understand about prayer and families. Really, they do. They're excited and they want to help. I mean, Christmas isn't very far away, and your baby is going to be arriving soon. They want you to be able to show

Will the beautiful centerpiece when he returns, even though the rest of the quilt won't be finished yet."

"I'm working on the tree now," Florence whispered. "But I'll keep stitching. Perhaps I can finish the border before Christmas."

"Then you'll say yes to the Frog Pond ladies?"

Florence nodded. "How can I say no to a circle of prayer surrounding our family? It only makes us stronger and united with one another. Tilly, you are wiser than you know. I thank you from the bottom of my heart."

When Dr. Rutler and Aunt Amelia came in, the two women were in each other's arms. They tiptoed past without a word and disappeared into the kitchen.

An hour or so later a watery sun broke through the clouds. *Journey mercies*, Florence mused as she nestled her bare foot into the warm fur on Vaughn's back. "Now Tilly will get a respite from the rain, maybe even dry her up a bit."

"I'm going out, too," Dr. Rutler said as he came into the room. "Aunt Amelia thought it would be nice if I'd cut a couple of nice fir branches to hang in the window. Or perhaps cedar. What do you think?"

"I'd like either one." Florence smiled. "It might be just what I need to instill a bit of Christmas into my heart."

"I'll do it, then." He looked at her searchingly. "Your eyes show weariness, and your cheeks are pale. Are you still taking your cod liver oil?"

"Yes," she replied. "Aunt Amelia won't let me forget."

"I didn't think she would. But I am going to suggest you lie down after lunch every afternoon. Once the baby arrives, you'll be up all hours of the night. It'll also prepare you for the delivery. It's hard on a mother to bear a child. You want to be fit for what lies ahead."

He strode whistling out the door as though eager for a touch of the sun and the sight of blue sky as the clouds blew past, hurrying as though they, too, chased the sunlight. It didn't take long for him to return. He stood at the edge of the porch, scraping the mud off his shoes.

"Mighty wet out there," he said as he pushed open the door. "Mud is almost knee-high in places it seems. And the grass, it's as slick as if covered with frost or a coating of ice, except it's only rain. But what a rain."

He set the boughs in the corner of the room and headed into the kitchen where Aunt Amelia waited. "I'm ready for my coffee and biscuits loaded with your wonderful apple butter."

"I'm sorry Dr. Rutler," she said. "I made scones instead, even found some lemon curd I didn't know I had. I warmed the apple butter on the back of the stove, too; seemed like it might be a nice touch on a cold winter day. I fixed a pot of tea, too."

"As long as there's coffee," he said as he returned to the front room. He handed the cane to Florence and bowed before her. "I've come to escort you to tea, my lady. May I take your arm?"

"Please," she replied, "I would be glad for your gentlemanly assistance."

They stepped into Aunt Amelia's kitchen as though they had the world on their fingertips. And true to Dr. Rutler's word, they really had come for tea. Aunt Amelia had managed to pull together an English tea, complete with tiny hazelnut cookies and bits of sweet chocolate alongside the buttered scones, apple butter, and lemon curd in dishes trimmed with sprigs of peppermint and lemon leaves. Even though Florence recognized the leaves from alongside the creek in the canyon, neither Dr. Rutler nor she would ever know how Aunt Amelia carried it off on such short notice.

They simply enjoyed. The spell wasn't broken until afterward, when Dr. Rutler announced that Florence needed a nap. "She needs to rest on her bed each day, Aunt Amelia. I'd be pleased if you made it part of her daily routine."

Although Florence fussed in her spirit, as she lay back on the pillows, she quickly relaxed. Sleep came softly, and she was shocked when she opened her eyes. The kitchen and the front room were quiet; the sun had disappeared, and dark gray clouds scuttled across the sky outside her bedroom window.

She sat up, put her feet on the floor, and reached for her cane. She pulled herself to a standing position then walked slowly through the door into an empty front room. Except it wasn't empty. A delighted gasp escaped her lips; the cedar boughs Dr. Rutler had brought in earlier now adorned both windows. Already they had decorated with the dried rose-hip garlands they had strung last year in the tent. Faye, in a playful mood, had once fixed icicles made of the strands of gray mosses into a beard to decorate her chin. They now dangled from the green boughs where the paper birds from last year's tree proclaimed a new version of Christmas cheer. There were even several of last year's birds' nests filled with nuts and dried berries tucked inside the fragrant branches.

"Do you like it?" Aunt Amelia asked as she came in from the kitchen.

"I love it," Florence said. "But I miss the candles. We still have them, don't we?"

Her aunt nodded. "I didn't have time to give the holders the extra rubbing they always need each Christmas. I'll do them later this evening. There'll be plenty of time."

Florence nodded. "Christmas is still several weeks away, and I'm still waiting."

"We'll wait together," Aunt Amelia said. "And when your time comes, I'll be at your side. I promise."

The days and nights passed slowly for Florence and her aunt. Each evening the two women sat together in front of the fireplace, Florence in the rocking chair embroidering the scripture to bind her prayers and hopes and dreams together and nourish her trust in the God she loved. It would join the border with the centerpiece, which the circle-of-love women continued to stitch.

Sometimes Florence wondered if some of them brought it home at the end of the day to stitch and pray through the night, for it was almost always then she most needed prayer. It seemed as though the December wind blew stronger, and the old-growth firs soughed their ancient song high overhead as though their hearts were bursting. Sometimes she fought back tears as loneliness overwhelmed her, at other times she prayed: Will, our baby, Aunt Amelia, Clarence, Tilly and Faye, Dr. Rutler, the Moads and the Bakers, Hal and Irene and little Maud, and gradually their names mingled together and disappeared as sleep overtook her.

"He giveth unto His beloved sleep," Aunt Amelia had said, and Florence slept through the night while the winds increased and rain poured out through a hole in the sky and dumped torrents of water upon the sodden Willamette Valley.

In the morning, Florence stood against her cane in front of the window, wondering how the animals had fared in the night and wishing with all her being she could be there for them instead of Aunt Amelia taking on the task. If only, but she had to wait.

Christmas was coming, and Will would be home. He'd hold her hand as the pains of childbirth wrenched her body. Together they'd pray and cling tight to each other. Through prayer they would grow closer together, not unlike the two saplings that sprang from one stump in the canyon. In the distant past, the old tree had been struck by lightning, but there was still life left in it. The saplings grew from the stump and became one of Faye's favorite places to play. Florence had found her there early one morning between the two young trees. As those trees had grown, they'd grown close together.

Faye named them Marian and Marion, "my twins," she'd say, and there she'd stand on one foot in the narrow space between them with her young firm arms wrapped around both of them. She said she whispered her stories to them, and then they'd clap their boughs and bounce in a passing breeze. Florence smiled. They were bouncing now.

And so was Aunt Amelia. A gust of wind, and she burst through the door. "It's terrible out there, and I don't know what we'll do." She slid out of her coat and untied the scarf wound around her neck and head. "You can hear the creek from the top of the hill. It's all brown with runoff and roarin' its head off. I don't know how we'll get out if we need to go anywhere. And it's almost Christmas Eve. I dare say we won't have any guests comin' our way in this rain."

"But we have everything we need," Florence protested. "The rain barrels are full and so are our cupboards. Please don't worry, we'll be all right."

"But will we?" Aunt Amelia asked. "What if you go into labor? How am I goin' to get a message to Dr. Rutler? How—"

"You'd have to go out through the swale and the back woods and knock on Arnold's door. He'd be more than glad to run an errand for Franklin's adopted granny. You know he would. And don't worry. You can always take Vaughn with you. He knows the way."

Aunt Amelia scowled. "I guess I could, but you can't say it would be easy. But I could, I guess I could."

Even as her aunt spoke, a pain gripped Florence's back. She gasped aloud as her abdominal muscles tightened. Her cane fell to the floor. She grabbed the windowsill with both hands and held on with all her strength as Aunt Amelia rushed to her side.

"I think you're going to have to go now," Florence whispered. "I think it's already begun."

18

W̲hen did this start?" Aunt Amelia asked. "I need to know."

"A twinge of pain woke me early this morning," Florence confessed. "And then it came again when I came into the front room and found you'd gone out into the storm to feed the animals. I'm sorry I didn't say something as soon as you got back, but I know first babies take their time to come into the world. And I—I wasn't sure if it was the real thing or not. I'm still not sure."·

Aunt Amelia nodded. "We can't take any chances, with the weather so bad and standing water everywhere. There'll be floodin', too. I'll take Callie and head across the garden and swale, see if I can find Arnold. But first, I'll put extra padding over the sheet to protect the bed, then I want you to get into a clean nightgown and lie down."

Florence did as her Aunt Amelia said, but it was hard to relax. She kept thinking of Will. Had he been delayed by swollen rivers and creeks? "Lord," she whispered, "bring my man safely home. I—I need him, dear Jesus. Help him keep his promise."

Aunt Amelia came back to her room. "I added wood to the fire and saddled Callie. There'll be plenty of water when we need it. We're ready to go now." She leaned forward, bowed her head, and put her hands on Florence's head. "Heavenly Father, our precious Lord and Savior, this girl is mighty precious to me and so is the little one she's carryin'. She needs her Will right now, too. And so does this baby. Please give him journey mercies and speed him on his way home so he can be at her side like he promised he would. Amen."

Then she was gone. The door slammed shut behind her.

"I wish I could see her riding Callie with her skirt pulled high and feet in the stirrups followed by Vaughn," Florence whispered. She shook her head. Even with her bent toward picturing things, she couldn't imagine her aunt riding astride their small mare. And in a dress, at that.

For a little while Florence dozed, then she wakened suddenly, the pangs of childbirth upon her. Agonizing pain swept through her, and she set her teeth as panic rose inside her. How could one struggle on when pain stole her breath and made it hard to breathe? Her fingernails dug into her palms, and even in her pain, she felt a sense of wonder. Her fingers were more limber than they'd been in weeks. The pain in her knuckles seemed almost gone.

Then suddenly—like part of a dream—Will was beside her. His touch on her cheeks, her chin, and her lips was gentle as if she were as fragile as the tender mayflowers deep in the forest in the springtime. She clung to him then, but gradually relaxed.

"Will, you kept your promise. Our baby's coming—and I'll do better with you here," she whispered. "Oh, Will, Will, please stay. Don't leave me alone again."

"I'm your husband," he whispered. "For better or for worse, I will not leave you or our baby. We'll get through this together. You have my word."

As the afternoon wore on, the pains grew closer and more regular. Sometimes they lasted longer. She caught herself holding her breath then, but Will's hands steadied her. Vaguely she was aware of Aunt Amelia's presence; heard her say to Will, "I'm glad you're here. I felt bad leaving her here all alone, but I had to get someone to go for Dr. Rutler. We needed him."

And then, through a blur of pain, she heard the good doctor's voice. She tried to say something, but could only cry out in agony. There were no words.

"Work with the pain, my dear," Dr. Rutler instructed. "Your baby is turned just right. You can push now."

She bore down with all her might as she clung to Will's hand.

"Your baby's almost here!" Dr. Rutler exclaimed. "Just go with the pains and push again. I see the top of its head."

She lay back panting, gathering her strength.

"Don't quit! It's almost here. Now again. Push."

"It's a girl!" Dr. Rutler exclaimed. "And she's beautiful."

Florence heard the snip of the scissors, and then Will laid her daughter wrapped in a towel across her chest. The baby wailed and waved her tiny arms as the exhausted mother touched her nose, her cheeks and soothed her with gentle words. "You're all right now, Sweetie. You're here with us, your very own mommy and daddy."

Will reached forward and touched her finger. Her little finger curled around it. "You already have a name, little daughter. You're Elizabeth Anne Nickerson, born December 21, 1899, at 4:12 p.m."

"Except," Florence said, "she's too small for such a long important name. I'm going to call her Beth, at least until she grows a bit."

"So am I," Will said. "It fits her just right."

Christmas Eve came to the cabin softly. It lingered in the doorway as it noted the table covered with a white cloth drawn close to a fireplace where coals glowed and flames licked the log within. Candles in the window nestled among cedar boughs shone joy, as did the three candles in the center of the table. Together they flecked golden light into the shadowed cabin room holding the sweet presence of Jesus, the Savior of the world, who came so long ago as a helpless baby wrapped in swaddling clothes, lying in a manger.

But this evening, an infant girl would sleep in a basket bundled beneath the star-covered quilt Mrs. Moad had made for her. The large star in the center would speak of a double meaning. First, the Star of Bethlehem that led the wise men to God's anointed Son. Second, and more important, the truth of the Bright and Morning Star, the One who led us all to God.

The blanket suspended between the front room and the bedroom parted as Will came into the front room with his beloved Florence cradled in his arms. He settled her onto the sofa and leaned forward to kiss her soft lips.

"I love you, Will," she whispered, and her lips trembled. "I've needed you so, my darling. Having you with me when little Beth came into the world was the crowning glory of my year."

"What about our wedding day?" he teased. "The day it all began."

"I know. But this was the ultimate joy, having you with me, holding my hand so tightly, and whispering encouragement into my ear. That was when your sacrifice eclipsed my pain. No more waiting, no more doubts or fears. You were there when I needed you most, and it was beautiful."

Vaughn trotted at Will's heels as he went back into the bedroom and returned carrying their new baby. He set the basket on the sofa close beside Florence and turned to her. "Aunt

Amelia left us a wonderful spread," he said. "I didn't have to do much of anything. She did it all before Dr. Rutler carried her off to Tilly and Clarence's for their Christmas celebration."

Will disappeared into the kitchen, as Florence looked around the room, noticing for the first time the red velvet runner beneath the candles, and the water buckets on the floor below the windows where candles tucked among the fir boughs shed Christmas cheer throughout the room. She smiled. *The loving care of Aunt Amelia and Will says it all,* she thought, *and I am blessed.*

The meal Will placed on the table was all Florence imagined it would be and more: bread-and-butter pickles, cranberry sauce, and pickled beets. His second trip added fluffy mashed potatoes, brown gravy, green beans with bacon and onions, and Aunt Amelia's famous hot biscuits served with fresh butter and strawberry jam. Topping it all off was a platter of juicy, sliced roast chicken to make Florence's mouth water.

With hands clasped and heads bowed, Will gave thanks to the God who had so faithfully cared for the wife he had left behind. "She is Your crown, Lord God. And little Beth, why, she's Your pearl. Thank You for this wonderful meal for our first Christmas together as a family. We praise You for what You are doing in our family and what You will continue to do. Thank You for this food. Bless Aunt Amelia for preparing it for us. Now bless it to our bodies to use and us to Your service. Amen."

After their meal, Will cleared the table. The decision to have Christmas pie on Christmas morning was made when little Beth whimpered from her basket. Will brought in a fresh diaper and laid the squirming baby in Florence's lap. She changed her as Will hovered protectively near. When she finished, he helped her place the hungry infant to her breast.

"She's so beautiful," Florence whispered as she suckled the infant. "Will, her eyes are wide open and she's looking at me. And guess what? Her eyes are as blue as yours!"

"It doesn't mean they won't darken later. My mother always said that's what usually happens." He smiled. "But I'd rather she had your brown ones, my darling. I really do."

"We'll have to wait and see. Praying and waiting and learning to trust. It's what I've been doing these many months." She changed the subject abruptly. "I have a Christmas present for you, Will, and I can't wait much longer to give it to you. I—I made it myself—sort of—but not really. You'll see."

"I have something to give you, too. It's not much but, well, you can go first. I need to learn to wait, too." A big smile flashed across his bronzed face, and Florence noticed for the first time the fine new lines rayed out from the corners of his eyes.

Tears blurred her eyes. *He missed me as much as I missed him,* she thought. *But, God, I don't want to go there. Tonight is ours. We need to handle it with care.*

"I'll blow out the candles in the window," Will announced, "and then do the dishes."

Florence heard him whistling softly as he went into the kitchen.

"It's just the way I imagined it would be," Florence said after their babe lay peacefully sleeping in her basket. She smiled as Vaughn crept close and lay as near to the basket as he could get. "It's time for our gift exchange. Except I need for us to sit so we're facing each other. Part of your gift is best displayed on the back of the sofa; the rest of it is in the packet with my sewing materials. Could you bring it in, please?"

Will smiled. "That I can, and I promise not to look inside." Instead, he leaned over and pulled her closer.

"Will," she teased, pushing his arms away, "I need the basket."

He grinned and strode back into their bedroom to get the basket she'd asked for. He set it on the floor beside her and watched as she removed a packet and put it on her lap. He sat down beside her, and she reached for his hand.

For a moment, she sat still, searching for just the right words. "I'll guess I'll begin with my dream the night Tilly gave me the verse about a tree growing out of a dead stump at the scent of water.

"In my dream was a Tree of Life quilt. But this quilt had a centerpiece, a map of our farm with a tree to almost fill it. Remember the night you described the farm you had bought? Well, the centerpiece had it all. There were birds and nests tucked in branches, a pool of water with a shiny dipper tied to a branch."

Her hand tightened under Will's, and he gently lifted it and touched it with his lips.

She continued. "Do you remember the lavender mayflowers, my mother's pink roses? Well, they were in my dream and so was the water dripping over mossy rocks into a pool surrounded by maidenhair fern. I saw deer and coon tracks, a squirrel scolding high in the tree. There were also giant maples and vine maples, and the silver dipper swinging from a limb. And a frog—I mustn't forget the frog."

She took a deep breath and sank into the pillow against her back. "I'm ready now to show you the centerpiece, even though it isn't finished. But it will be soon."

She told him about Tilly, Aunt Amelia, and Martha, and how they'd helped her, described to him the circle of love and the dear women who stitched, each stitch a prayer, each stitch a hope that drew their hearts together and to the heart of their Lord.

Will unfolded the centerpiece slowly. He looked up and she saw wonder in his eyes. Tears, too. They slid down his cheeks, glistening in the candlelight.

"And now you need to unfold the border so it reaches across the back of the sofa. It's in the top of the basket," Florence said.

He did as she requested and began to read the scripture as he tenderly fingered the dark green silken stitches she had striven so hard to perfect: "There is hope of a tree, if it be cut down, that it will sprout again, and that its tender branch will not cease."

He turned to her. "You did this yourself, didn't you?"

She nodded. "There's more, Will. I'm going to include parts of the entire three verses so it encircles the entire quilt. The ladies already have the Tree of Life pattern they're piecing together for the rest of it. I also want to include more pictures in the centerpiece. Perhaps a cabin, the face of a mountain lion. And Vaughn has to be in it, too, his head thrown back, his front paws braced against the stump. But most of all, I want to include mother's pearl necklace at the top of the tree pointing to Jesus above all, king of our hearts and king of our home."

"It will be a beautiful heirloom for our family," Will said. "It's a design God gave you for the generations to follow. My darling, God has blessed us above all we can ask or imagine."

Once again, she was in his arms as he carried her into the bedroom. He kissed her tenderly as he drew the quilts around her shoulders.

"Tonight you gave me the gift of your heart," he said, "symbolized with a work of art from your hands. In the morning, I will give you my gift, the one I found in the hills of Washington State. You already have my heart, but tomorrow you'll receive it so you'll remember forever."

"Until then I'll wait," she whispered. "Will, I think I'm finally learning."

19

Florence awakened at morning's first light when Will slid out of bed. He dressed, then hurried to the kitchen. She turned onto her back and listened. In a few minutes, she heard the sound of iron on iron as he lifted the stove lid and put kindling in the kitchen stove followed by larger pieces of wood. Soon the scent of hot coffee, followed by the warmth of the fire, would move through the rooms.

She moved onto her side and smiled. She had lain facing her husband most of the night, their hearts and bodies touching, their arms entwined around each other. But when in the darkness baby Beth started to cry, Will had awakened quickly. He'd scratched a fingernail over a match head, using it to touch the candle beside the bed. It sprang to light and pushed the darkness into the corners of the room.

Remembering his willingness to get up and change baby Beth and then tuck her into her arms for the midnight feeding touched her deeply. Truly Will was proving how much he loved her and their child. Still, she couldn't help but wonder if he would ever tell her the details of why he had left her and stayed away so long without writing.

But he had returned. He'd kept his promise—she knew deep inside her heart—he deserved her trust. "I'd like to hear his story just the same, Lord," she whispered, "Please make it soon."

But first, there would be breakfast. Then Will came into the bedroom carrying the silver tray loaded with cups and saucers, utensils, a pitcher of cream, and an entire apple pie.

"I'm taking you at your word," he said as he set the tray on the stand by the bed. "Apple pie for breakfast. We'll save the pumpkin pie for tonight in front of the fire." He reached out and touched her hand. "Can you wait until evening for your gift? I'm making something special to go with it, and it's not finished yet."

"Take as long as you need. I can wait," she said softly. "But we do need coffee."

He nodded. "I'll be right back with the pot."

True to his word, he returned and set the pot down. Taking her hands in his, they bowed their heads. Their grace was a simple thank-you rising from hearts too full to say more.

When they lifted their heads and smiled at each other, they knew their hearts beat in unison.

Later in the afternoon while Florence rested with her sleeping daughter tucked in the curve of her arm, Will slipped in and sat down on the edge of the bed.

"I think right now I feel like you did last night when you said you didn't know where to start when it was time to give me the gift you were making, not only for me but for our children and our children's children."

Her hand reached out and grabbed his. She held it tight and waited.

"First of all, Florence," he continued. "I want to thank you for trusting me and allowing me to leave you, and you with child and alone, to right a wrong that had somehow become a part of my story."

"Which is my story, too," she whispered. "Oh, Will, I love you, and I truly don't expect you to be perfect. And like you said to me once—at least I think it was you—you said, 'Just begin at the beginning and I'll listen.' I'm listening now."

A faraway look clouded Will's eyes. "It all started when I lost my pack horse, Comet, when she leaped from the trail into Dead Horse Valley, that awful graveyard filled with the bones of pack animals that gave up and jumped over the cliff. When I looked down and saw my mare dead in the valley, I didn't want to go on. But I did write to you about it before we were married, and you lived in the tent, didn't I?"

Florence nodded. "Sometimes the stories in our life need to be retold," she said softly. "It's all right to tell it again. I'll listen."

Will shook head. "You amaze me, Darling. Really you do. Well, anyway, I sold my supplies on the spot to prospectors on the trail who were eager to buy right then and there. Once my grubstake was gone, I hiked back to Skagway with enough money in my pocket to buy a ticket to Seattle. I knew I'd have to get a job when I arrived if I was ever to get back to the settlement. And I did.

"For several weeks I worked off Schwabacher's Wharf loading and unloading the supply ships. It's where I met Carl. He said he'd worked there since the steamboat *Portland* docked there in '97 with its ton of gold. It was then that Seattle became known as the gate to the Klondike.

"Carl and I became a team. We worked well together; the boss man said we were the fastest and best loaders and unloaders on the wharf. It was backbreaking work, but the pay was good. Then Carl came up with an idea. When he asked if I'd team up with him to help him herd a bunch of horses to winter at a remote ranch in eastern Washington, I jumped at the chance. We'd split the pay between us.

"That was enough for me. You know me and horses, we were on our way, and we had a great time finding our way through remote valleys and up hills we hadn't even known existed. I liked it a lot better than the docks, and Carl did, too. But it didn't last. Something bad happened. I didn't realize until after we'd been paid and were headed back to Seattle—Carl had a gambling problem. Having so much money on his person made him nervous, so he asked me to take most of his pay and keep it for him until he got back. He just didn't trust himself.

"He left for town alone for a shave and a haircut but never returned. When I went to town to look for him, no one could say they'd seen him. When I went back to camp, I looked through his things to see if he'd left a note. There was nothing. Instead, I found a wad of bills in my saddlebag. I wished I could have returned the money to him, but I couldn't. And now, it won't happen."

"Is Carl connected to the man I saw watching me from the bushes? Are they both a part of your story?"

"Yes, they are." He frowned and his lips tightened. "I found out later he was Carl's older brother. You actually met him before I did."

"I'm sorry, Will. I still don't get the connection. What was his name?"

"Ray, short for Raymond. Ray came looking for me, hoping I knew where Carl was, but he saw you instead. Only later did I find out he was Carl's brother, but it was after he helped you at the cabin."

"Later, we talked. You see the police found Carl's body in a ravine not far from our camp. That's when I became a suspect in the eyes of the law. But after Raymond had done some sleuthing on his own, he didn't think they had enough proof to come to the conclusion I had murdered my partner and made off with his money."

Florence shook her head and sighed. "There were no witnesses—only a body? Will, I don't understand."

"I don't understand it either and neither did Ray. When we talked at the feed store, I told him I wanted to clear my name. That's when he suggested I go with him to Seattle when he came back through so I could tell my story to the authorities. You see, Ray had seen the card shark who lost the last card game to Carl and took his money. Oddly enough, the crook did look quite a bit like me."

"And since you and Carl had worked together, they suspected you had stolen it, then disappeared," Florence added. "Is that the way it happened?"

Will nodded. "Ray learned his brother was dead and that the police believed I was the card shark who had stolen his money, murdered him, then dumped him in the ravine. After that he did some checking on his own. Then he talked to the sheriff and told him I'd just returned from Skagway—the card shark had never been in Alaska or Canada, only in Oregon and Washington. But it still didn't help clear me. After all, they were still convinced I was a murderer and a thief. It's why Ray came to look me up. He wanted proof and was determined to get it. You know the next part of the story."

A sudden light dawned in Florence's eyes. "He told me he was looking for a Mr. Nickerson who sometimes went by the name of Nick."

"You didn't know I sometimes used the name Nick, short for Nickerson. It wasn't until later, when I talked to Ray at the feed store and found out he was Carl's brother, that I tried to give him the money Carl left with me. He wouldn't take it. He felt that since there were no witnesses, I should go back to Seattle with him to talk to the police there."

"But what good did you think you could do? Will, I don't understand."

"Neither do I. Except my father told me never to bring shame to the good name of Nickerson. I knew I hadn't done anything to hurt my friend Carl. And Ray believed me."

"So what happened when you went back to Seattle with him?"

"When I told the authorities I didn't do it, they still didn't believe me. Even though they had no concrete evidence I was guilty, they put me in jail. That's why I couldn't write again. I couldn't bear the thought of you receiving a letter from an inmate in a prison cell.

"Several weeks later, Ray talked them into releasing me so we could look for witnesses, perhaps someone who had been at the tavern the night Carl had been seen with him there. The sheriff took a chance and told us to go, and we did. Well, actually, they had an officer accompany us. But we didn't mind."

"Oh, Will. I daresay underneath they knew what kind of man you were. But I have another question. How did you know you would be here for the birth of our baby?"

"I just knew I didn't do it, Florence, so I asked God to fight for me and set me free. And He did. We even found the man they said looked like me—and Ray was right, he did. The card shark who was cheating and stealing and lying, and finally killing, proved to be the real thing, and I, the counterfeit. Only God had the power to prove it to the police.

"There was nothing left for me to do—except brave the rains and the high water and head on home. I had to walk the horse I'd rented in Oregon City through the creek the night I arrived. I was wet clear to the skin, but I didn't even feel the cold.

"I had to be there for you, Florence. I had to keep my promise."

Will and Florence talked the afternoon away until the sun disappeared leaving behind a world washed clean and bright in the glory of sunset. Will had gone out to finish whatever it was he wanted to finish and left her nursing little Beth.

Florence lay still, her head propped on a pillow, her arm encircling her baby. Lying there, she felt both comfortable and comforted. Will was no longer under the weight of the possibility of being arrested as a killer and a thief. Their baby had arrived, and she herself, although still suffering some of the symptoms of rheumatic illness, was regaining the use of her hands and experiencing less pain. Nor had she suffered any problems following childbirth.

She heard the door open and lifted her head. Will pushed back the blanket. In one quick movement, he was beside the bed touching her hand. "You're beautiful with your dark smoky hair spread out on the pillow, Florence, and your new-mother look makes your skin glow." He sat down beside her and buried his face in her hair. "Are you ready for your surprise?"

Her own hand reached up and touched his hair, his cheek. "More than ready," she whispered. "I've waited a long time for this moment, but now we have to wait again. Our little one is nursing and we mustn't wake her."

It was Will who gently removed their daughter's lips from her mother's breast. Moving slowly so as not to waken baby Beth, he eased her into her basket and carefully tucked the star quilt over her. She took a deep breath. Her tiny rosebud mouth quivered in an almost smile, and then she settled into sleep. Florence reached for her pillow and placed it against her back so she could sit comfortably on the edge of the bed at Will's side.

"Carl and I were on our way back to Seattle, heading through a narrow canyon when I saw something flash gold on the rocky ground. Right away, I stopped and dismounted and there it was, a heart-shaped locket made of gold, just waiting for me to pick it up."

Will continued. "As soon I saw it, I knew it was for you. But once I was here, I wanted to make a special box to put it in to forever whisper my love." He reached beneath his coat, drew out a small wooden box, and placed it in her hand.

"Why, Will, it's beautiful!" she exclaimed. "I had no idea you could carve like this." Her fingers traced the exquisite rose he had so carefully carved on the lid.

"Open it," he said as he helped her lift the clasp.

She gasped. There lying on a tiny square of red velvet lay a gold locket with a delicate gold chain.

"Take it out, Honey. Open it."

She did even though her fingers fumbled; it opened, and there before her was Will's dear face. Tenderly, she touched the tiny photograph. A flood of love brought tears to her eyes as he placed the locket around her neck.

"You and our Lord are the keeper of my heart," he whispered. Then he kissed her.

The emotion she felt threatened to make her tears flow. She was Will's wife, and it was everything she'd ever wanted. "More than anything, Will, I just want to be home with you, cooking your meals, raising your children, quilting your quilt."

He took her hand tightly in his and nodded toward the window. "The firs are soughing tonight. They're singing your dancing song."

She laid her hand on Vaughn's silky head and looked out the window to watch the tree branches moving to a light breeze. And Will was right, they were singing her dancing song. It was a promise. "You shall go out with joy and be led forth with peace. And the trees of the field will clap their hands."

She laid her head on Will's shoulder. One day soon, they would dance with the wind and the trees. It was their song, and all they had to do was wait.

Discussion Questions

1. Aunt Amelia gave Florence a blessing when she was on her way to her wedding. In what way, verbal or otherwise, did your own parents or spiritual leaders give you a blessing when you told them you were about to be married? Do you think a blessing given at key points in your life made a difference and is this something you want to do for your own children? If so, what would you say?

2. Although Florence is thrilled to marry Will, she feels a certain sadness. Her dreams of getting married when the roses were in bloom would never be fulfilled. What did Aunt Amelia and her sister-in-law, Opal, do that brought joy to her heart? What has brought joy to you even when your most cherished dreams weren't fulfilled in the manner you expected?

3. Today friendships are hard to develop and communities don't come together as they did in the past. Family, friends, and neighbors helped Florence in her time of need. What can we do to strengthen relationships within our neighborhoods?

4. Will voiced feelings of inadequacy as he compared the Moads' beautiful home with the rustic cabin he built for Florence. How does she encourage him? How do you encourage your loved ones when they are feeling doubts and fears about themselves?

5. How did Florence cope with her feelings of helplessness after facing the mountain lion? What do you do when you are faced with a situation you have no power to change?

6. Aunt Amelia and Tilly often brought gifts of food from their kitchens to Florence when she was feeling poorly.

Can you remember a time when you were encouraged in this way? Is there, in turn, someone you can help?

7. Will shows his love to Florence by making things for her with his hands. Aunt Amelia cooks food in her kitchen. Tilly drops by to chat and to help with chores. In what way do you show your love to those you care about?

8. Chronic illness changes everything. Have you been affected by a serious illness? Have you ever served as a caregiver for a family member, friend, or neighbor? How did it affect your life?

9. When Will chose to bring the dog home, he did so without consulting Florence. How did she handle this? Has someone you love made decisions without asking you to be a part of the decision-making process? How did you react?

10. Vaughn turns out to be a special encouragement to the entire family. Tell us about a special pet in your life.

11. As a child, Florence lost her parents. Because of this, she feared being abandoned by people she loved. How did she face her fear when Will left for Seattle, leaving her to fend for herself? How did prayer and trust in God help Florence through her pregnancy without Will?

12. Have you ever felt alone and abandoned? How did you respond? What advice would you give to someone who feels this way?

13. Florence often turns to the Bible for words of comfort. How did scripture support her through the events that were to follow? Has God ever used scripture to prepare you ahead of time for a trial you didn't know was coming? What verse in the story touched you most deeply, and how would you like God to use it in your life?

Want to learn more about author
Eva J. Gibson and check out other great
fiction from Abingdon Press?

Sign up for our fiction newsletter at
www.AbingdonPress.com
to read interviews with your favorite authors, find tips
for starting a reading group, and stay posted on what
new titles are on the horizon. It's a place to connect
with other fiction readers or post a
comment about this book.

We hope you enjoyed *A Stitch and a Prayer* and that you will continue to read the Quilts of Love series of books from Abingdon Press. Here's an excerpt from the next book in the series, Tara Randel's *Rival Hearts*.

1

Molly Henderson forced herself to remain still, even though every fiber in her being wanted to scoot to the end of the chair and rattle off at least twenty questions that came to mind. "A challenge?"

Her boss, imposing as he sat in his leather chair behind an enormous mahogany desk, steepled fingers under his chin. Self-satisfaction curved his lips. "Let's call it a little in-house competition between you and Ben. The winner will be editor-in-chief of my new magazine, *American Legend*."

Pushing her glasses higher on her nose, Molly's gaze darted to Ben Weaver, the man who had just gone from colleague to competitor. His veiled expression showed no emotion. Was he as surprised as she? Of all the topics this meeting could have entailed, informing them of a competition hadn't been one of them.

She'd been surprised by the impromptu call to the boss's office. Equally surprised when she found Ben waiting to attend the same meeting. What a way to start her Wednesday morning.

"My plan is unusual, I know. Both of you are qualified for the position and would do an excellent job." He shrugged. "I decided to put my own spin on the promotion process."

Putting his own spin on things had made Blake Masterson a very successful publisher. His unorthodox style of management set him apart in the publishing world, but somehow it worked for him. Mid-fifties, self-made, and very popular in the Tampa Bay area for his publicity stunts. The stunts captivated the public but always brought notice to charitable organizations and needs in the community. The man had a savvy mind and knew how to use it to keep his company in the limelight.

"As you know, Master's Publishing is ready to expand with a new magazine. I need people focused for the long haul to get the magazine up and running and to handle day-to-day operations afterward. You have both proven valuable in your current editorial roles, and I want to see where this challenge will take you."

Molly bit back a sigh. She'd been with Master's Publishing for eight years now, four as senior editor and writer for *Quilter's Heart Magazine*. She loved working for the company, but steered clear of Mr. Masterson's publicity stunts. She had seniority; her longevity alone should give her first shot at the position. But a competition involving her? Honestly, she'd never been very good at any endeavor outside her comfort zone, which consisted of working behind the scenes or immersing herself in a quilting project. Given the determined look on her boss's face, his grand plan would definitely be uncomfortable for her.

But not for her soon-to-be rival.

She sneaked another peek at Ben. Tall, built, tan, and extremely masculine. Not to mention the most soulful brown eyes she'd ever seen. Yes, the man was handsome. But his ego? Another story all together.

They'd rubbed each other the wrong way since the first day he stormed into Master's Publishing six months ago to take over as senior editor and head writer of *Outdoor Adventures Magazine*. He'd smiled his confident smile and acted like he owned the place. He assured Mr. Masterson his former freelance writing and television experience would increase circulation of his magazine and far outsell all the other magazines published by Master's, including "the little quilting magazine," as he referred to Molly's magazine. He made friends with all the staff, frequently took over meetings, and whenever she tried to make suggestions, he smiled down at her, not taking her seriously. She never let on how much he bugged her, but boy, did he bug her. And now a competition? Ben would relish any out-of-the-box trial thrown his way. This was so unfair.

"I've been very impressed with both of you. Our sales have increased due to both your efforts, and we've already made a presence with our digital editions.

"Ben, before you took on *Outdoor Adventures*, I was ready to pull the brand, but the articles are entertaining and well-written. The results have increased the circulation and advertising revenue. Of course, your past foray into the cable television show *Extreme Survivors* helped ramp up circulation. After watching you on TV, I jumped at the chance to lure you onboard. Nothing like having a mini-celebrity on staff."

Yes, Molly knew that part, since everyone in the office talked about him.

Mr. Masterson grinned, as if Ben's fame would benefit him. "I allowed you to fulfill your prior commitments when you first took the job, but since the traveling has wound down, we're happy to have you in the office full-time."

Some people, Molly thought.

"I have to give credit to Charlie," Ben said as he leaned back in his chair. "He kept the magazine going while I finished up my schedule."

"Always good to have a competent assistant, especially one who knows what readers want. Since you've shown your dedication, I thought you might want a shot at the new position."

"Yes, sir, I would," he said, his smile dazzling.

"Good. Good." Mr. Masterson turned to Molly.

"Molly, you've been here since you started as an intern. When you came up with the idea for a quilting magazine, I have to say I wasn't convinced the market could sustain it. But you kept after me and proved me wrong. Who knew crafts were so popular? You've built a readership, and the numbers keep growing, but you haven't quite gotten to the place where readers connect you with Master's Publishing.

"Your monthly Dear Reader column is great, but it's time to take your relationship with your readers to the next level. I know you're working on a special project to connect with readers, but let's up the ante. Get them behind you."

Which Ben, with his high profile in the extreme sports world, had already done in just six months.

"Even though both magazines are regional, as editors, I'm sure you'd like to work on a bigger project like *American Legend*. You both have a knack for finding in-depth human-interest stories to touch your particular readers. Just the type of content I want for my new magazine. Stories featuring ordinary people doing extraordinary things in their lives—not expecting accolades—just doing what comes naturally. I want stories of daring-do, faith-based stories, tearjerkers whenever possible. You'll be given a chance to shine as an editor as well as moving up in the company."

Rumors had infiltrated the office for weeks now that Mr. Masterson had something in the works. Speculation about the new magazine ran the gamut from parenting advice, to the auto industry, even a new comic book division. With Mr. Masterson's love for giving back to the community, *American Legend* was a perfect choice for his reputation. And while Molly appreciated the idea, she still had questions.

"Could you be more specific?" she asked, still unsure about her part in this latest development. "About the challenge?"

With pen and paper in hand to jot down notes perhaps affecting her future with the publisher, she waited patiently. She loved being an editor, loved her magazine. But a promotion? Who wouldn't jump at the chance?

"Out of all our inventory of magazines, both of yours are the most popular. Top sellers, actually. And polar opposites. So I thought, why not have my two top editors switch places. Molly, you belong to a quilting group, right? The one you've mentioned in your column?"

"Right."

Mr. Masterson turned to Ben. "You will join Molly's quilting group. Let's find out if those outdoor skills of yours translate into sewing and producing a well-made finished product."

"Quilting?" Ben raised a questioning eyebrow.

Oh, her friends would love this. Her boss had no idea of the dynamics in an all-female gathering. Ben might be used to his rough and tumble world, where strength and experience with Mother Nature gave him the upper hand in the wilderness. Spending an hour with suburban moms who talked about love, life, kids, what to make for dinner, and what their husbands were in trouble for might send him screaming into the sunset. She'd seen the caged look on many faces of men forced to spend too much together time in a room with chatty women. Ben didn't know it yet, but he'd just signed up for an adventure very few men could withstand and survive to tell the tale.

"Right now you're working on the next issue of *Outdoor Adventures* which features . . ." Mr. Masterson glanced down at his notes. "Kayaking?"

"Yes."

"Perfect. Molly—"

Please, please, please, not sports. No physical activities. Anything but the outdoors. Her pulse rate elevated, and she held her breath while she braced herself.

"—we'll get you hooked up with a local kayaking event. Since Ben already has some activities lined up for the next issue, here's a perfect opportunity to show me what you're made of."

"Kayaking?" Molly croaked, echoing Ben's earlier response to his challenge.

"Afterward, we'll showcase your individual journeys in your magazines." Mr. Masterson shot them a teasing wink. "I do love publicity. And friendly competition."

Molly gripped her pen. Friendly? More like a battle of the sexes if you asked her. One she doubted Ben would make easy. He took on a challenge the way an explorer took on the jungle: divide and conquer. No way could she kayak a few feet from shore, let alone with some major activity cooked up by Ben. She doubted she could get in the thing without tipping over.

"You'll each have four weeks to complete your tasks. At the end of the month, I'll review your progress and name the new editor-in-chief. Any questions?"

Ben spoke up first. "Yes, sir. Where will my new office be located?"

"Your office?" Molly sputtered.

He smiled at her. "Yes. My office."

"Don't you mean *my* new office space?" she countered.

Mr. Masterson stood. "Both of you follow me."

He led them down the hallway from his office. All the offices on this floor were for upper management, while one story down housed the other departments, including her office and Ben's. Once they reached their destination, Masterson stood to the side as he opened the door with a grand flourish. Ben, his eyes bright with success, motioned for Molly to enter ahead of him. The more confident he appeared, the more steamed she became. No way would she let him win.

The vacant office had more square feet than both Molly's and Ben's current offices combined. Wide windows overlooked downtown Tampa, offering a glimpse of the vast city spread out before them. Bright sunlight glinted off Tampa Bay, where boats zigzagged across clear azure water. From a closer view, eleven stories below, cars moved in a steady stream of traffic alongside a city park dotted with benches located under palm trees and plenty of grassy area before ending at the banks of the Hillsborough River.

Standing before the windows, Molly savored the sunshine and forced herself to calm down. Her inside office had no windows, while Ben had managed to procure an outer office with one window. What she wouldn't give for this spectacular view every day. .

Ben might be Mr. Masterson's bright, shining star, but Molly had grown tired of working her tail off with little reward. As much as she loved *Quilter's Heart,* lately she'd been antsy. Ready for a change. A challenge would shake up her life, hopefully in a good way. And the best outcome? To beat out Ben for the job.

She turned just in time to see Ben place his briefcase on the empty desk, remove a clear plastic cube with a baseball inside, and set it on the smooth surface. His gaze met hers, telling her with no words necessary he'd marked the place as his. She bit back a retort because their boss hovered in the doorway, but she vowed to make him eat those unspoken words.

"Before you two plan your individual battle strategies, I suggest you return to your desks and figure out the logistics of the challenge." Mr. Masterson motioned for them to exit the office. "I'll stay in the loop to see how you're both progressing. I may want to tweak things a bit as the competition heats up."

Bad enough she had to compete, but knowing Mr. Masterson might throw in a game changer somewhere along the line? Great. Just great.

Being dismissed, Molly walked on shaky legs, allowing Ben to precede her. He couldn't know how her boss's grand scheme, or Ben's confidence in assuming he'd won the challenge before it had started, rattled her. Never had she imagined she'd have to prove herself in such an unusual way. She'd been a loyal employee for years. Had doubled the circulation of her magazine in her time as editor. Shouldn't her work ethic have merit in her boss's decision?

She joined Ben by the elevator, tugging the lapels of her jacket over her blouse. Her mind ran in so many different directions, she couldn't focus on any one thought. She glanced up to watch the progress of the elevator as numbers lit up above the door, trying to ignore the hunky man who now worked against her. Ben hadn't said much after the question in Mr. Masterson's office, and the silence grated on her sensitive nerves. Finally, he turned her way.

"Do you have anything planned right now?"

"Just heading back to my office."

"Mind if I tag along? We can discuss the challenge details."

Details. Right. If only she could ignore him like she wanted to. Suspicious, she asked, "Why my office?"

He chuckled. "Either will do. I thought you might be more comfortable hammering out the details on your own turf."

Oh, sure. Now he decides to be accommodating, unlike his confident assumption he'd be moving into the upstairs office. "Fine."

The elevator doors parted, and Ben nodded for her to board first. He entered, pressed the button for their floor, and the doors slid shut, followed by a jerk of movement.

Molly stared at her fuzzy reflection in the metal doors. Why did these things always feel so small? And why did Ben have to stand so close? His shoulder brushed hers, but she held her ground. No way would she shy away from him.

Instead, she tapped her foot to the canned music playing some oldie but goodie.

"Something wrong?" he asked.

"No. Just enjoying the music."

"You're off beat."

She stopped. Stood stiffly. "Guess we all can't be good at everything."

He chuckled again.

The close confines made her antsy. When the doors opened, she hoofed it to her office. Once inside, she relaxed. Her turf indeed.

To one side, a comfy arm chair and end table neatly displayed the most recent issues of *Quilter's Heart* magazine. Along the opposite wall, a long table held a sewing caddy with her quilting supplies and an assortment of folded fabric on top. Fresh potpourri scented the air. As she closed the door, the busy sounds from the office diminished. She smoothed her skirt and took a seat behind her desk, adjusting the desk calendar containing daily scriptures.

Her domain. Her little place in the vast world of publishing. Small as it might be, everything was neat and tidy, in its place, just the way she liked it.

Until Ben walked in and stirred up her senses with a mega-dose of testosterone.

Why did she let him get to her? He'd grabbed her attention right from the first day they'd met, thinking how fun it would be to work with a handsome, world-traveling guy. Until he opened his mouth and ticked her off. Since then she'd done her best to ignore him, but right now, his very male presence in her very female office had her hormones in an uproar.

Hiding her reaction from Ben, she pulled her best business face and motioned for him to take a seat in the chair before her desk.

His large hand pulled the chair back a few inches to make room for his long legs. Today he wore a pastel blue button-down shirt with navy slacks and loafers. Almost like he knew to dress up for the meeting since he usually wore more casual, athletic clothes to the office. But he didn't know about the meeting, so of course, he couldn't have planned his wardrobe.

And did he have to smell so good? His sandalwood cologne had distracted her from the moment she took a seat next to him in Mr. Masterson's office, just as it did now.

Stop.

With a flick of her hand, she centered her pen and pad on the desktop before brushing her hair from her shoulder, waiting for him to speak.

"So what do you think about Masterson's idea?" he asked, as he lowered himself into the chair.

"I think it's crazy."

He waved a hand. "Yeah. I know Masterson likes his stunts, but even I have to admit the idea is a little out there. He doesn't usually involve his employees."

"Guess we're his guinea pigs."

Ben's eyes flashed humor. "You up for a little challenge?"

What did he mean? He didn't think she could handle an outdoor challenge? She didn't miss the way his gaze took in her wavy blond hair, brown-framed glasses and body curves. Okay, her glasses might present a functional problem and she could shed a few pounds, but those minor obstacles didn't mean she couldn't complete the challenge.

"I'm as up to it as you are," she asserted, a little miffed and on the offensive. "I want the job."

"So do I."

"Do you plan on sticking around to see the outcome?"

"What do you mean?"

"It isn't a secret you love to travel. What's different now?"

He took a moment to answer. Sorrow flashed across his strong features, gone just as quickly as it came. "I have my reasons."

"Ben, I've been here a long time. I'm the face of stability. Can you make the same assertion?"

"You don't know what I bring to the table."

"Exactly. Does anyone?"

His eyes narrowed, humor gone.

"Wouldn't it be easier for all involved for you to step back and let me, the person with seniority, take the position?"

"Yes. Very easy. But I don't like easy." His steady gaze met hers. "We're competitors."

His predatory smile sent goose bumps over her skin. She recognized the look, had seen it right before he jumped off a cliff into churning water or let out a yell as a parasail took him high above the ocean. Yeah, she watched television, too.

"Look, Ben, I may not seem like an outdoorsy kind of girl, but I can be pretty single-minded when I want something."

"Yeah?" He chuckled. "No offense, but when was the last time you spent any time outdoors?"

"And I could ask, when have you ever sewn anything?"

His gaze focused on the wall behind her head as he thought. "About a year ago. We were camped in the middle of nowhere in the Australian outback. The canvas tent ripped in a freaky windstorm, and I had to repair it with some spare fishing line."

Of course he did.

"Not the same as stitching with a fine needle and thread on much more delicate fabric."

He shrugged. "I'll adapt."

Wouldn't he just.

Well, so would she. She hadn't grown up with overprotective parents not to have the backbone to reach deep down and go after the editor-in-chief position. Hadn't she been proving herself all her life? It seemed like it, especially when her accomplishments were always secondary compared to a brother who excelled at everything he did.

Her gaze settled on Ben. Not much different from now.

For all her bravado, she'd worry about the actual challenge itself later. After she Googled kayaking and figured out what she'd been forced into. First, she needed to make Ben believe he had something to worry about.

Before she had a chance, he stood, as if ready to leave, when he noticed her partially completed quilt top draped over the quilt rack in the corner. He walked over. "It looks like a jigsaw puzzle."

She grinned. He wasn't far off in his assessment. "I can see why you'd think so. There aren't enough pieces stitched together yet to make the pattern discernible."

"So what's it going to be?"

"The pattern is called Hearts Entwined." She grabbed a picture from her desk and handed it to him. The pattern, so romantic in her mind, would show even more beautifully when she finished the piece.

On a white background, separate geometric shapes of triangles, squares, and diamonds in dark red came together to form a heart. The same shapes in pale pink formed another heart.

"If you look at the colored fabric, you'll see once the pieces are stitched together, it resembles two hearts inside each other, the red one right side up, the pink one upside down. With the contrasting colors, it looks like hearts entwined."

A narrow, deep red border surrounded the heart shapes, making them stand out. The piece would be finished off with a wide white border with matching red and pink squares in the four corners. She hadn't yet picked out a fabric for the backing, but she'd get to it soon.

He tilted his head. "Yeah, I can see. Clever."

She couldn't resist a smile. Most guys would have just agreed to placate her, not taking a good look at the intricate pattern to see the design. Knowing how Ben operated, getting down to the nitty-gritty of most things, she shouldn't be surprised by his interest.

"Are you working on this?"

Joining him, Molly ran her fingers over the soft material. "Yes. It's a special project I came up with for the next *Quilter's Heart* issue."

"How so?"

"Every year I make a quilt and auction it off at the local Charity Expo held in the beginning of May. I got an idea to have my readers send in a piece of fabric holding emotional significance to them, along with the story to go with it. Once the quilt is finished, I'll showcase the finished piece and the stories from my readers in *Quilter's Heart*. This way they get to be part of the quilting experience. Then it'll be auctioned at the Expo."

He looked at the fabric swatches on the worktable. "Looks like a lot of work left. It's already the beginning of April."

"I'll finish," she assured him. Or herself, anyway. With everything going on in her life lately and the challenge thrown into the mix, she would indeed cut it close.

After putting out a reader all-call for fabric six months ago, material had trickled in. She thought her idea might be a bust and worried she'd made a colossal mistake. Once the deadline approached, however, a deluge of fabric arrived at the office. With more than enough to complete the project, Molly had begun cutting out the pattern and started stitching the pieces together by hand. Then, two weeks ago, she'd had to stop.

An organization she volunteered for, Second Chances, faced a disaster. A kitchen fire in the facility where women of domestic abuse trained for jobs had sustained major damage. Thankfully, the shelter, which housed women who had eluded their abusive partners before transitioning their lives, had escaped the fire. Between the burned-out kitchen and smoke damage, Molly and others had been working at the center to move what they could to another donated location and keep the programs going during construction to get the center back to normal. She just now had time in her schedule to get back to the quilting project.

"It's a nice idea." His deep, brown eyes focused on her. "So will I be working on this quilt?"

Horrified, Molly's eyes widened. "No way."

"No need to get touchy."

"You'll be working on whatever my group is sewing."

He glanced at the quilt-in-progress and frowned.

"Thinking sewing a tent might be a piece of cake, right now?"

"I'm thinking our boss is a very shrewd man. Admit it. We've both got a big learning curve ahead of us."

"Maybe."

"Most definitely." Ben caught her gaze. "I don't suppose your quilting group will be easy on me?"

"Not any easier than me getting the hang of kayaking." She held back a sigh. "With the Expo next month, I've got to get busy."

He turned back to the quilt top. "You'll finish in a month?"

She masked the concern in her voice. "I'll get it done." Worried or not, she wouldn't let Ben see any weakness.

"I'll be the first to admit making a quilt looks pretty complicated, but when was the last time you participated in any sporting activity?"

"It's been a while."

"Right." The grin again. "So I have a proposition."

She regarded him with suspicion. "Which is?"

"How about I give you a head start? Then you can begin getting used to the kayak so when you have to succeed in your part of the challenge, you don't die on me."

Her cheeks grew hot. "First of all, I won't die. And second, I don't need your help."

"The boss said we can figure out the details between us." He eyed her from head to toe again. "I can afford to help you out."

Okay, his comment had her steamed. "How generous of you," she snapped.

"I'm a generous kind of guy."

"As much as I appreciate your offer," she said as she opened the door to see him out, "I'm going to decline. Once you get started quilting, you'll be wishing *I* gave *you* a head start."

He might *think* he had the advantage, but with his attitude, she'd show him her spunky side. If anything in her life made her want to step it up and prove she could master the challenge, his words sealed the deal.

Ben bit back a chuckle. Miss Molly thought she had it under control. He'd let her keep thinking she had a shot, right up until the boss appointed him editor-in-chief.

He sauntered back to his office. Who knew Molly had a backbone? A pretty solid one from what he could see. By her refusal of a head start, he had no doubt she wanted the new position as much as he did and would work hard to win. He'd never seen her assertive side before. Even though he hadn't had the opportunity to work with her on any projects, he had seen her around the office. And most of those times she'd been quiet, busy with her tasks, but he'd taken notice of her. Unassuming, but she'd caught his eye. Now he has the chance to find out more about the real Molly.

Ever since returning to Tampa, he hadn't yet renewed any old friendships or made new ones, in or out of the office. After a cycling accident in France eight months ago, he'd decided to step back from the television show. His injuries—massively scraped up arms and legs along with a sprained wrist and con-cussion—were not life threatening, but enough to keep him on the sidelines for a few weeks when his recuperation didn't fit into the filming schedule. When the camera crew moved on to the next location, Ben found himself abandoned in a foreign country. Alone. He hadn't liked it one bit.

During the downtime, he had an epiphany. He wanted a change in his normally hectic life. His parents had loved to travel, taking him on grand vacations from Alaska to Fuji from the time he could walk. They were the ones who encouraged him to pursue his dreams. After their deaths, he'd still trav-eled but stayed away from Tampa and the memories of a happy childhood swimming and boating in Florida waters. By refus-ing to settle down, he'd missed out on having a support sys-tem. Friends he could call on in an emergency. It couldn't have been any clearer than while he recuperated in France.

Traveling had become old hat, losing its appeal and challenge with no one to share it with. He was thirty-five, with no permanent home. No people in his life to depend on. Much as he tried to make it work, his television crew couldn't take the place of family. A high-profile position for the new magazine would allow him to put down roots. Reconnect with childhood friends he saw too infrequently. Instead of running, he wanted to come home. A sense of permanence. Miss Molly was not going to keep him from getting what he longed for.

"Hey, Ben. Got a minute?"

Charlie, Ben's assistant editor came up beside him, a folder in his pudgy hands. Slightly overweight, sporting glasses and thinning hair, he didn't resemble an athletic type of guy, but he sure knew the business of sports and publishing. He could recite statistics from the Super Bowl, World Series, or Stanley Cup in his sleep.

"Sure. What's up?"

"I've been going over scheduling for the next issue," Charlie said as he followed Ben into the office. "I've confirmed a kayak excursion for this month. I can assign a writer who will cover the story and interview the participants."

He couldn't have asked for more perfect timing. "You don't need to find a writer."

"What are you talking about?"

"I have someone lined up."

Charlie waited a beat before asking, "Who?"

"Molly."

"Molly." Charlie's round face scrunched up in confusion. "You mean quilting Molly?"

"She's the one."

"You want to run that by me again?"

He explained the challenge Masterson has just issued.

"So, Molly will be taking up kayaking." Charlie blinked. "I just can't see it."

Neither could Ben, but who was he to argue? It was evident from the boxy jackets Molly wore to hide her curves, she didn't exercise much. It didn't matter—he liked her look. Her wavy, shoulder-length hair and the ever-present glasses covering intelligent blue eyes gave her a studious air he found attractive. She had a passion for quilting, a quick mind and, as he'd learned today, an even quicker tongue. But at the same time, her apparent lack of athletic ability gave him an advantage. If she trained hard enough, she might be able to pull it off. But he doubted it. In fact, he depended on it.

"And you have to take up quilting?" Charlie asked.

"Yep."

While Molly's office held all sorts of quilting doodads, sporting equipment littered Ben's. A bow and arrow stood in one corner, camping essentials he hadn't had a chance to sort through since returning to Tampa dumped in another. Paperwork piled up on his desk. Paperwork he'd intended to get to before the call to the morning's meeting with Masterson.

Sunlight streamed through the window. Even though his office was tiny, Ben couldn't help feel a little guilty he managed to get space with natural lighting while Molly's work space resembled an oversized cubicle. No wonder she wanted the big office upstairs. And from the way her eyes had narrowed when he placed his prized baseball on the empty desk, he may have stirred up more in Molly than he bargained for.

Taking a few more minutes to give Charlie more details on the challenge, he saw doubt in his assistant's eyes.

"Do you even know how to sew?" Charlie asked, still puzzled by Ben's part of the challenge.

"I'll figure it out. How hard can it be?"

"It's sewing," Charlie stated as if Ben were dense.

"Yeah. So?"

"I don't know any guys who sew."

"You will now."

"Okay, so what if you win? What happens then?"

"Not if. When," Ben told him. "If you play your cards right, buddy, you might end up in this office."

Charlie glanced around the room, a sly grin curving his lips. "Think I'll get promoted?"

"Why not? You've been working with *Outdoor Adventures* long enough to take over my job."

"I'm liking this challenge more and more."

"Don't get ahead of yourself. I have to win first."

Charlie tossed the file on Ben's desk. "With you in the driver's seat, all I have to do is sit back and enjoy the ride."

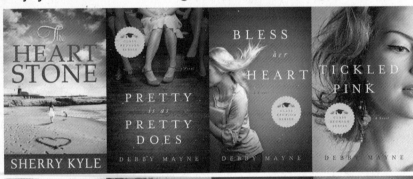
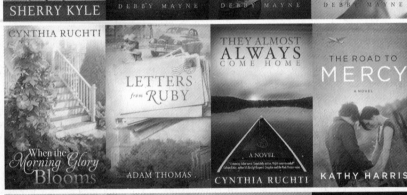

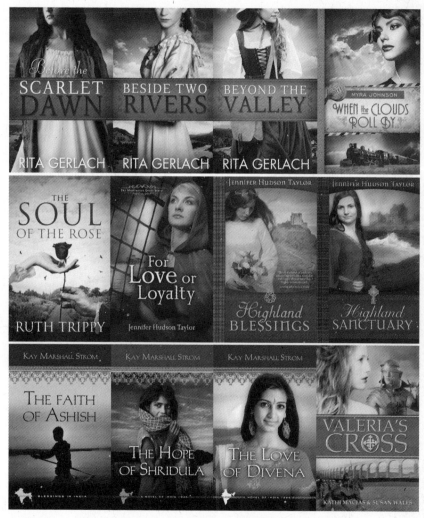

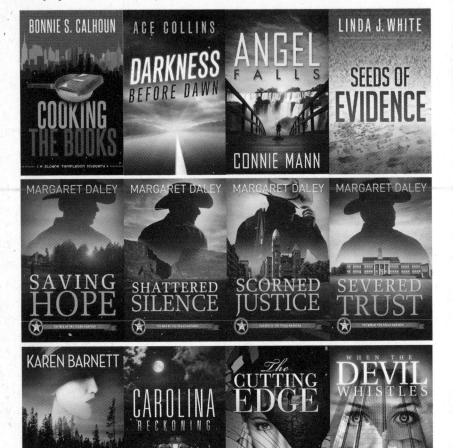